'We have, in von Schirach's ice-cool, effortlessly classy prose, an antihero accused of murder, who sees the world in too-vivid colour, and his bumptious defence lawyer, who sees everything in shades of grey. It makes for a disconcerting mix of build-up and anti-climax, tension and humour, lies and truth, and a novel as intriguingly eccentric as its protagonist' Alison Flood, *Observer*

'Written in a beautifully understated style that matches his protagonists' detached and rather abstract view of life ... It's an examination of the disconnection between truth and reality that is tantalising and disturbing in equal measure' Laura Wilson, *Guardian*

'Ferdinand von Schirach is one of Europe's most celebrated crime authors ... This is a sophisticated novel about a man whose emotional detachment is as chilly as it is destructive' Joan Smith, *Sunday Times*

'Ferdinand von Schirach's prose is elegant and unemotional ... the story is intriguing and often disturbing' Marcel Berlins, *The Times*

'This centaur of a story, half-study of the alienated artist with a traumatic past and half-portrait of the lawyer as cantankerous philosopher of truth, may baffle or frustrate crime buffs. Other readers will enjoy its free and quizzical approach to genre expectations – and the swift, clean, enigmatic prose that Anthea Bell translates with her flawless grace' Boyd Tonkin, *Independent*

'This is an effective riddle of a novel. Details accumulate, tensions build and misdirection abounds, while Anthea Bell's crisp translation accentuates von Schirach's cool, pointillist prose ... Perhaps the only secure verdict the novel delivers is that its author is one of the most distinctive voices in European fiction' Christian House, *Daily Telegraph*

The Girl Who Wasn't There

FERDINAND VON SCHIRACH

Translated from German
by Anthea Bell

ABACUS

ABACUS

First published in Great Britain in 2015 by Little, Brown
This paperback edition published in 2015 by Abacus

1 3 5 7 9 10 8 6 4 2

Copyright © Ferdinand von Schirach and Piper Verlag GmbH, Munich 2013
Translation © Anthea Bell 2015

The moral right of the author has been asserted.

A CIP catalogue record for this book
is available from the British Library.

ISBN 978-0-349-14046-9

Typeset in Aries by M Rules
Printed and bound in Great Britain by
Clays Ltd, St Ives plc

Papers used by Abacus are from well-managed forests
and other responsible sources.

 MIX
Paper from
responsible sources
FSC
www.fsc.org   FSC® C104740

Abacus
An imprint of
Little, Brown Book Group
Carmelite House
50 Victoria Embankment
London EC4Y 0DZ

An Hachette UK Company
www.hachette.co.uk

www.littlebrown.co.uk

As soon as the light of the colours
green, red and blue
is mixed in equal proportions
it seems to us to be white

Hermann von Helmholz on colour vision

On a fine spring day in the year 1838, a new kind of reality was created on the Boulevard du Temple in Paris. It changed human vision, knowledge and memory. Ultimately, it changed the truth.

Daguerre was a French theatrical designer. He wanted to create scenery that looked like reality itself. He let light fall on iodized silver plates through a hole in a wooden box. Mercury vapour made what was in front of the box visible, but it took the silver salts a long time to react: horses and pedestrians moved too fast to be shown, movement was still invisible, the light left a record only of buildings, trees and streets on the plates. Daguerre had invented photography.

In his 1838 photograph, the figure of a man is clearly visible in the formless shadows left behind by the movement of carriages and people. While everything around him is in motion he stands still, his hands clasped behind him. Only his head is blurred. The man knew nothing about Daguerre and his invention; he was a passerby who had stopped to have his shoes cleaned by a bootblack. The apparatus was able to make a visible record of the bootblack and his customer – they were the first two people to appear in a photograph.

Sebastian von Eschburg had often thought about that motion-less man and the way his head was dissolving. But only now, only after everything had happened and the course of events could not be reversed, did he understand that the man was himself.

Green

1

The village of Eschburg is halfway between Munich and Salzburg, a little way from the major roads. Only a few stones of the castle up on the hill that once gave the village its name still stand today. An Eschburg had been Bavarian ambassador to Berlin in the eighteenth century, and when he came back he built the new house beside the lake.

The last time the Eschburgs had been rich was at the beginning of the 20th century, when they owned a paperworks and a spinning mill. In 1912 the first-born son and heir drowned in the sinking of the *Titanic*. Later, the family had felt a little proud of that. He had booked a first-class cabin, and was travelling with his dog as his only companion. He had declined to get into a lifeboat, presumably because he was too drunk.

His younger brother sold the family firms, speculated, and lost most of his fortune during the crash of the 1920s. After that, there was never enough money to renovate the house properly. Plaster flaked off the walls, the two side wings were not heated in winter, and moss grew on the rooftops. In spring and autumn metal buckets stood in the attics to catch the rain.

Almost all the Eschburgs had been hunters and travellers, and for two hundred and fifty years they had filled the rooms of the house with the things they liked. There were three umbrella stands made of elephant feet in the entrance hall, and mediaeval boar spears on the walls – long lances used for hunting wild boar. Two stuffed crocodiles lay locked in combat on the upstairs landing; one had lost a glass eye, and part of the other's tail was missing. In the domestic offices, there was a huge brown bear with almost all the fur worn away from his belly. The horned heads of kudu and oryx were mounted on the library walls, and the head of a squint-eyed gibbon stood on a shelf there between busts of Goethe and Herder. Beside the hearth lay drums, natural horns and lamellophones. Two grave, black figures, African fertility gods made of ebony, sat either side of the billiard room door.

Icons of saints from Poland and Russia hung in the corridors, next to enlarged postage stamps from India and Japanese ink drawings. There were little Chinese wooden horses, spear tips from South America, the yellow fangs of a polar bear, the head of a swordfish, a stool with the four hooves of a sable antelope, ostrich eggs, and wooden chests from Indonesia to which the keys had long ago been lost. One guest room contained fake Baroque furniture from Florence, in another there was a glass-topped showcase full of brooches, cigarette cases, and a family Bible with a silver lock.

Right at the back of the park there was a small stable with

five stalls. Ivy grew on the walls and grass between the paving stones in the yard. Paint was peeling off the shutters, rust had turned the water brown. Firewood was drying in two of the stalls; tubs for plants, salt for the paths and fodder for game were stored in another.

Sebastian came into the world in this house. His mother had intended to give birth in hospital in Munich, but the car had been standing out in the cold too long and wouldn't start. Her labour pains began while Sebastian's father was still trying to get the ignition to catch. The pharmacist and his wife came up from the village, and Sebastian's father waited in the corridor outside his wife's room. Two hours later, when the pharmacist asked if he wanted to cut the baby's cord, he shouted at the man that the starter was no bloody good. Later he apologized, but in the village they wondered, for a long time, what that portended.

Not much attention had ever been paid to children in Sebastian's family. They were taught how to hold a knife and fork properly, boys learned to kiss a lady's hand, and they were told that as far as possible children should be seen and not heard. Most of the time, however, no one took any notice of them. Sebastian was eight when he was allowed to eat with his parents for the first time.

Sebastian couldn't imagine living anywhere else. When he went away with his family in the holidays, he felt strange in the hotels where they stayed. He was glad to come home and find everything still there: the dark floorboards in the corridors; the worn stone staircase; the soft afternoon light in the chapel, which didn't stand quite straight.

There had always been two worlds in Sebastian's life. The retinas of his eyes perceived electromagnetic waves between 380 and 780 nanometres, his brain translated them into two hundred tones of colour, five hundred degrees of brightness and twenty different shades of white. He saw what other people saw, but *in his mind* the colours were different. They had no names because there weren't enough words for them. His nanny's hands were cyan and amber; his hair, as he saw it, shone violet with a touch of ochre; his father's skin was a pale greenish blue. Only his mother had no colour at all. For a long time Sebastian thought that she was made of water, and took on the shape that everyone knew when he went into her room. He admired the speed with which she always successfully performed this transformation.

When he learned to read, the letters had colours too. 'A' was red, like the village school-teacher's cardigan, or the Swiss flag that he had seen on the mountain hut last winter: a fat, strong, unmistakable red. 'B' was a much lighter tone: it was yellow and smelled like the fields of oilseed rape he passed on the way to school. It floated in the room above pale green 'C', it was higher and friendlier than dark green 'K'.

Since everything had not just its visible but also its other, invisible colour, Sebastian's brain began putting that world into order. Gradually he created a map of colours with thousands of streets, squares and alleys, and every year a new level was added to it. He could move about that map, he found his memories through the colours. The map became a complete picture of his childhood. The household dust was the colour of the time he spent in the lakeside house: a dark, soft green.

He did not talk about it; he still thought that everyone saw in the same way. He couldn't stand it when his mother wanted him to wear brightly multi-coloured sweaters; he would fall into a rage, tear them to pieces or bury them in the garden. Finally he got his way, and was allowed to dress solely in the dark blue jackets that were the usual rustic garb of the district. Until he was ten years old they were his daily wear. In summer he sometimes wore a cap just because it was the right colour. The au pair girl guessed that Sebastian was different. He commented on it when she wore a new perfume or a different lipstick. Sometimes she called her boyfriend in Lyons. She spoke French to him on the phone, but she felt as if Sebastian understood that foreign language, as if the sound of her voice was enough for him to know what she was saying.

At the age of ten Sebastian went to boarding school. His father, his grandfather and his great-grandfather had been to the same school before him, and as the family no longer had enough money for the fees, he obtained a scholarship. The school sent a letter to his home, saying exactly what clothes every boy was to bring with him, how many pairs of trousers and pyjamas, how many sweaters. The cook had to sew numbers into all his clothes, so that the school laundry could keep the children's things separate. When she brought his trunk down from the attic, the cook cried, and Sebastian's father told her crossly to stop making all that fuss, it wasn't as if the boy was going to

9

prison. She shed tears all the same, and although the letter expressly forbade any such thing, she packed a jar of jam and some money among his clean shirts.

The cook wasn't really a cook; it was a long time since the Eschburg family had employed any domestic staff. She was one of the family herself, a distant relation, some kind of aunt, and in better days she had been the housekeeper and lover of a German consul to Tunisia. The consul died without leaving her anything, and she was glad to be taken in by the Eschburgs. Sometimes she was paid a salary, but usually she simply got free board and lodging.

When Sebastian's father took him to the boarding school, the child would have liked to take the white water-crowfoot flowers floating on the lake with him, and the wagtails and plane trees from the front of the house. His dog was lying in the sun, his coat was warm, and Sebastian didn't know what to say to him. The dog died six months later.

2

Sebastian was allowed to sit in the front seat of the car on the way to his boarding school because he felt sick in the back of the old vehicle on long drives. Looking out of the window, he imagined that the world was only just being created, and hoped that his father wouldn't drive too fast, or it wouldn't be finished in time.

Once past the orchard on the banks of the large lake that his father called the Swabian Sea, they reached the Swiss border. The area between Germany and Switzerland, said Sebastian's father, was no-man's-land. Sebastian wondered what the people of no-man's-land looked like, what language they spoke, and indeed whether they had any language at all.

The border official looked dignified in his uniform. He checked Sebastian's new passport, he even asked Sebastian's father whether he had anything to declare. Sebastian stared at the official's pistol in its shabby holster, and was sorry that the man didn't have to draw it.

On the other side of the border his father changed some money and bought chocolate at a kiosk. He said you always had to do that when you crossed into Switzerland. Each square of chocolate was separately wrapped, and the silver foil was stuck down with tiny photographs: the Rhine Falls at Schaffhausen, the Matterhorn, cows and milk churns outside a barn, Lake Zurich.

They drove higher into the mountains; the air grew cooler and they wound up the windows. Switzerland, said Sebastian's father, was one of the largest countries on earth; if you laid the mountains out flat, the country would be as big as Argentina. The roads became narrower; they saw farms, the towers of stone churches, rivers, a mountain lake.

As they drove through a village that looked particularly neat and tidy, Sebastian's father said, 'Nietzsche lived here.' He pointed to a two-storey house with geraniums on the windowsills. Sebastian didn't know who this man Nietzsche was, but his father said it so sadly that the name stuck in his mind.

They drove for about another thirty kilometres through the rocky landscape, and finally parked in the marketplace of a small town. Because they were a little too early, they went for a walk along its streets. The town had houses two or three storeys high, with tiny windows, arched gateways, and thick walls to keep the hard winters out. From here they could see the school buildings, part of a Baroque monastery. Arcades surrounded a fountain dedicated to the Virgin Mary, and the two towers of the mighty Collegiate Church rose beyond it.

They were met by the principal of the boarding school, wearing the brown habit of a Benedictine monk. Sebastian sat on the sofa beside his father. There was a Madonna behind glass in a niche in the wall. She had a tiny mouth and sad eyes, and the baby in her arms looked unwell. Sebastian felt uneasy. He had a bird-whistle in his trouser pocket, along with a very smooth stone that he had found on the beach last year and the remains of some orange peel. As the men discussed things that Sebastian didn't understand, he picked the orange peel in his pocket apart into ever tinier pieces with his thumb and forefinger. Once the grown-ups had finished talking at last, and Sebastian could stand up, his father said goodbye to the monk. Sebastian was going to shake hands with the strange man too, but the monk said, 'No, no, you're staying here now.'

The tiny scraps of orange peel had dropped out of Sebastian's pocket; they were scattered on the sofa, and there were dark patches on the upholstery. Sebastian's father apologized, but the monk laughed it off. It wasn't as bad as all that, he said. Sebastian knew that the strange man was lying.

3

Life in the monastery had concentrated on reading and writing for centuries. The library was a high-ceilinged hall with light oak floorboards, and it contained over 1,400 manuscripts and over 200,000 printed books, most of them bound in leather. In the eleventh century the monks had founded a scriptorium, and they had added a printing press in the seventeenth century. For the school students, there was another library, a room with dark wooden tables and lights with brass lampshades. Among the boys, rumours circulated about secret rooms in the monastery cellars full of banned books: accounts of torture and witch trials, manuals of sorcery. The Fathers did not actively encourage reading; they knew that many boys would come to it of their own accord, and others would never find books interesting.

In the seclusion of the monastery, Sebastian began reading. After a while the boarding-school rules no longer bothered him, he got used to saying Mass morning and evening, to lessons, sports and study periods. The rhythm of the monastic days was always the same, and it gave him the peace and quiet to live in the books.

*

For the first few weeks, he missed the house by the lake. The boys were not allowed to go home except in the holidays. Telephone calls had to be booked in advance. Every other Sunday Sebastian called his home. He stood in one of the little wooden cubicles in the entrance hall of the monastery, and the Father on duty at the gate put his call through.

On one of those Sundays it was his mother who answered the phone. Sebastian knew at once that something was wrong. His father was ill, said his mother, but not seriously. When Sebastian hung up, his knees were trembling. Suddenly he was convinced that only he could save his father. To do that, he would have to walk alone through the Viamala Ravine. Sebastian was afraid of the ravine, the darkness there, the narrow way along it. He had not gone on the class excursion to see the place. *Via mala* meant 'the bad way': walls of rock three hundred metres high, smooth and cold, stone steps and bridges.

Sebastian set off at once, without telling anyone. He took the bus from the boarding school. Only after setting off did he realize that he was wearing thin indoor shoes and had not brought a jacket. He was twelve years old, he was afraid of heights, but he must do it. He walked very slowly. When he crossed bridges he kept in the middle of the path and did not look down. He heard the river below him. He was so pale that other people out walking asked several times whether they could help him. After three hours he had done it. He went back to the monastery. They had been looking for him, and of course the monk who bore the title of Prefect didn't understand about his father. Sebastian was chastised, but he didn't mind: he had saved his father's life.

*

16

The school was almost two thousand metres above sea level, winters there began early and went on for a long time. It was late autumn before they turned any heating on; the tall rooms were never really warm, and there were draughts in the long corridors. Sebastian was always glad to see the first snows fall. Then sleighs were brought up from the cellar, and the boys went skiing at weekends. In the mornings there was a thin layer of hoar-frost on the quilts of their beds, and tiny icicles came out of the taps in the bathrooms.

Sebastian was unwell every year at the beginning of winter, when he would develop an inflammation of the middle ear and a high temperature. The village doctor had a large diagram of the middle ear in his surgery. He showed Sebastian the skin, cartilage, bones and nerves in this diagram. Perhaps the skin of his ears was too thin, the doctor suggested. Gleaming chrome instruments lay on his desk; they were cold, and hurt when they were pushed into his ailing ear. Sebastian thought of the cook at home, who used to make him compresses of finely chopped onions to cure the pain. She said that onions made you cry, but they could do you good as well. The cook would sit on his bed and tell him about Tunisia, the spices on sale in the markets of the Medina quarter, the desert lynx that had ears with tufts like paintbrushes, and the heat of the Saharan wind that she called the *chehili*.

In the dark months at the boarding school, when books were no longer enough for him, when the nursery garden, the sports field and the benches were covered with snow, the colours in Sebastian's head were his salvation.

4

It was the first day of the long summer holidays. Sebastian had hardly slept. They set off for the game preserves at four in the morning. It had been raining overnight: the meadows were damp; earth stuck to their gumboots and weighed them down. Sebastian's father was carrying his double-barrelled shotgun over his shoulder. The stock rubbed against his loden coat where the fabric had worn thin with the years. The roses and gold lines of the English engravings on it were hardly visible, the stock itself was almost black. The loden coat smelled of rabbits and tobacco. Sebastian thought of the gun that his father had promised him when he took his hunting examination. He could take it when he was seventeen, so there wasn't long to wait.

He liked walking with his father. Hunting is a serious business, his father had often said, and Sebastian knew what he meant. It was different only when they were out on a shoot with beaters. Then there was potato soup in the yard of the hunting lodge, and it was all rather noisy. Often there were new guests, 'wild boar piglets' as the beaters secretly called them. They wore new coats and had new guns. The wild boar piglets were taken to special places where they couldn't do any harm with their guns. They talked all the time, even when they were waiting for game to turn up. They talked about their work in the city, or about politics or something else, and Sebastian knew that they didn't understand hunting. Later, when the kill was laid out in front of the hunting lodge, the animals were dead and dirty. Sebastian stopped going on shoots like that. But when they were alone, and his father hardly spoke, the forest and the game belonged to them, and there was nothing dirty and nothing wrong about it.

They climbed to the hide and waited until the morning mist had dispersed. When the roebuck came out into the clearing, Sebastian's father gave him the field glasses. The deer was a fine six-point stag, he was tall and proud, and very beautiful. 'We have plenty of time,' Sebastian's father whispered. Sebastian nodded. It was early August, and the close season wouldn't begin until mid-October. He wondered why his father had a gun with him at all if he wasn't going to use it. But then he thought that later on he would always bring his gun with him too.

His father produced a cigar from his cigar case; the leather was stained and old, just as everything that his father owned was old. From here they could see far down into the valley, to the tower of the village church, and on a clear day even further, all the way to the Alps. Later on, Sebastian would recall every detail: the cigar smoke, the smell of resin and wet wool, and the wind in the trees.

They took turns with the field glasses, which were so heavy that Sebastian had to prop his elbows on the crossbeam of the hide. They watched the roebuck for a long time.

Then his father briefly took aim and fired. They clambered down from the hide, and Sebastian ran across the clearing. The deer's forelegs looked as if he were still trying to run, they were at an angle and small, his eyes were open, bulging and clouded, his red tongue was strangely twisted. Sebastian knew the old jargon of hunters, who said 'lights' instead of eyes, and muzzle instead of mouth. His father had said that hunters were superstitious, and you mustn't use ordinary words in the forest for fear of warning the game. But now the deer was dead, and words made no difference any more.

His father bent over the animal, spread its back legs and knelt on them. He cut the abdominal wall from the anus to the throat, and blood and guts spilled out. His father removed the rumen, heart, spleen and lungs from the body and placed them on the grass beside him.

Sebastian felt as he had when he was out walking and had looked down into a ravine. He couldn't tear his eyes away from it. He had gone on staring down into the depths, defenceless, bereft of his own will, until his father had snatched him back from the brink. And now it was the cut that his father had made with his knife. It both attracted and repelled Sebastian. He couldn't move, he looked at the white parts of the deer's body, the muscle fibres and the bones. At last his father had finished, and put the deer over his shoulders. Sebastian carried the rucksack and followed his father back to the car. It was going to be a hot day, vapour was beginning to rise from the meadows, the light was glaring, and it was better to stay in the shade of the trees.

At home, Sebastian's mother was sitting out of doors at the iron table under the chestnut trees having breakfast, with her two dogs dozing on the lawn. It was Thursday, and she would be going to a horse show today; Sebastian had seen the horsebox. A few years ago his mother had had the stables renovated, and now her two dressage horses lived in them. Sebastian kissed his mother on both cheeks, then ran up to his room and took her present out of the case. He had made a nutcracker in the workshop at school, a nutcracker in the shape of a little man with white teeth, a red beard and a black hat with a wooden pheasant feather in it. Sebastian had spent a long time working on it, and had painted the feather brown and green. But now the present seemed to him silly. He looked down at the ground when he gave it to her. He still had resin on his hands from the hide, and now it stuck to the nutcracker because he hadn't handled it carefully enough. His mother thanked him. Twice, she made the nutcracker open its mouth. Then she went on reading her *Equestrian Review*. The registration papers for her horse shows lay on the table. Sebastian told her the news from his boarding school. Sometimes she asked a question without looking up from her papers. After a while she said that she'd better be going. She folded her napkin carefully so that the edges coincided perfectly. She kissed him on the forehead. The dogs jumped up and trotted down the avenue to the stables at her side.

Sebastian stayed sitting in the shade of the old chestnut trees. The long summer holidays lay ahead. Maybe he would go down to the boathouse and work on the wooden canoe, which could do with a new coat of paint. Sebastian remembered all three of them crossing the lake in the boat, his father rowing, while he lay on his front, chin propped on the gunwale. He had still been very young, maybe five or six years old. His mother had been wearing a pale linen dress, and she sat stiffly on the seat in the middle of the boat. She still used to laugh a lot at the time, and she squealed when his father splashed water on her with the paddle. Sebastian had dipped his hands in the cold lake, he had seen trout, perch and whitefish, and sometimes he could smell his mother's warm perfume: roses, jasmine and oranges wafting over the water.

All that seemed to him very long ago. He knew, now, that his parents did not love each other any more. He often looked at the album with their wedding photographs in his father's study. In those pictures, they looked young and strange, his mother diffident and soft, with a frank face and clear eyes.

In the past, when Sebastian's parents were still speaking to each other, he had often heard his mother telling his father that he had no ambition, no self-discipline, not even a proper profession. You needed aims in life, she had said, that was what mattered most.

Sebastian went to the garage for his bicycle, pumped up the tyres and rode out of the park. His friend lived in the last house before you reached the fields and, on seeing Sebastian, the boy's grandmother called out of the window to say he was down at the lock with the others. Sebastian turned his bike, rode back to the marketplace, and beyond the pharmacy turned into the path through the fields.

His friend was standing at the water's edge with the other village boys. Although they hadn't met for the last three months, they greeted Sebastian as casually as if he had never been away. They spent the day repairing their raft. It had been lying in the mud all winter, and the tree trunks it was made of had absorbed a lot of water, making them heavy and slippery.

They put unripe corn cobs on sticks and grilled them. The corn stuck in their teeth and tasted of nothing much, but the smoke of their fire drove the wasps away, and it was pleasant to sit beside it. They picked reeds, cut them up, and smoked them as if they were large cigars.

In the shadow of the alders, the lake was cool and dark. Sebastian swam far out and floated on his back. If he raised his head, he could see his family's house on the other side of the lake, shining bright white in the sun. He saw the landing stage there, the boathouse, painted blue, he heard the clear voices of his friends on the bank, and when he closed his eyes everything inside him turned to a single colour for which he knew no name.

Early in the evening Sebastian rode home, washed his face and put on clean clothes. It was too chilly to eat out of doors, and the cook had laid the table in the room with a view of the landscape. His father smelled of alcohol and looked tired.

'I'm not hungry, Sebastian, I'll just have something to drink.'

He's grown thin, thought Sebastian. He knew that his father was hardly ever at home, and spent most of his time on his game preserves in Austria. When he was here, he was almost always in his study. The curtains there were never drawn back, and no one could enter the room when he wasn't at home. He used to lie on the sofa, staring at the ceiling and smoking. He spoke less and less these days, his suits hung loose on him, and he was beginning to drink in the mornings.

After supper they went into the billiard room. His father was unsteady on his feet.

'Shall we have a game?' asked Sebastian.

'No, I'm too tired. You play and I'll keep you company.'

Sebastian arranged the billiard balls. His father sat on the window-seat with a glass of whisky and lit a cigar. Sometimes he looked at the billiard table, and said, in his old-fashioned French, '*entrée*', '*dedans*' and '*à cheval*'. Sebastian played an American break, concentrating hard; he drove the ivory balls along the cushion round the table. For a long time, the clicking of billiard balls on the cloth was the only sound.

When darkness fell, he replaced the cue in the wooden stands and sat down in an armchair beside his father. There was still a light on in the library; a narrow strip of it fell through the sliding door on to the floorboards. The wood looked like dark velvet.

'It's good to have you here,' said his father. His voice was colourless.

'Shall I put the light on?' asked Sebastian.

'No, please don't,' said his father.

Outside, a hawk screeched. Sebastian was feeling sleepy. He saw his father's profile in the semi-darkness, his high forehead, his hollow cheeks. He heard his father breathing. It seemed to him that his father wanted to say something, but was still searching for the words. However, his father said nothing.

*

Sebastian had fallen asleep in the armchair. When he heard it, he ran down the stairs to the main hall on the ground floor in the dark; he stumbled, grazing his knee, ran on down the passage to the study. He flung the door open.

The only light came from the lamp on the desk. A cardboard box of ammunition stood beside it, holding cartridges of shot with pale red cartridge cases, 12/70 calibre. Sebastian cautiously skirted the desk. His father's tweed suit had already worn thin at the knees and elbows, his green handkerchief was hanging out of the breast pocket of the jacket. His left leg lay on the chair, which had fallen over; the heel of his shoe was trodden down, showing the nails in it. His father had no head left. The force of the nine lead pellets had shot away his face and lifted off the roof of his skull.

Sebastian stood in the study, unable to move. He smelled the gunpowder, the whisky dripping from a bottle that had tipped over on to the stone slabs, his father's aftershave. He saw the dust on the books, the brass telescope, the cracks in the leather upholstery and the silver cigarette case with the big jade stone set in it. Then it was too much for him, images raced through his mind, were superimposed on each other, came together again and again in new combinations, he couldn't arrange them in any kind of order. Colours swelled to form huge blisters.

Sebastian's nose was bleeding; warm blood ran over his lips and on to his tongue. He took a step forward, picked up the cigarette case and switched the desk lamp off. He didn't know why he did that, but afterwards it was quieter.

'We have plenty of time,' his father had said.

5

He woke up in his bed. He didn't know how he came to be there. He was wearing his pyjamas. Downstairs, he heard his mother's voice. His mouth was dry. Getting out of bed, he went over to the window; it was already midday. There was a police car outside the house, and beside it a black station wagon with opaque glass windows.

The family's doctor came into his room. He said that Sebastian was not to exert himself, he had better lie down again and have a good long sleep. The doctor gave him a tablet and a glass of water, and then closed the curtains. Parrots were embroidered on the yellowish green background of the old fabric, magnificent birds with huge beaks. Sebastian tried to stay awake, but the birds blurred and dissolved into nothing before his eyes. He dreamed of the jungle. It was hot and damp there, too many colours, too many odours.

Later on the strangers were no longer in the house. All he heard were the sounds that had always been there: water flowing into the moss-grown well outside the house, the weathercock creaking every time a gust of wind blew, the marten up in the attic. Sebastian was cold, freezing; his pyjamas were drenched with sweat.

Next morning his mother came to sit on the side of his bed and held his hand. He couldn't remember her ever doing that before. She told him, twisting the ring on her finger, that he had had a bad dream, that was all, he'd been feverish. Sebastian looked at her mouth, at her lips that were pale and dry now. She said that a shot had accidentally been fired while his father was cleaning a gun. Her mouth went on moving, but Sebastian could hardly hear what she said. He felt as if a wall had risen between him and his mother. The wall was like the rough deckle-edged paper that his father always used to buy at the old mill on river a few villages away. Sebastian had once gone with him to see how it was made. A man had scooped the separate pages out of a trough with a sieve, and water had dripped on sheets of felt and seeped through them. The paper was made from cotton waste, said the man in the blue apron; it came from the hospital.

Sebastian wanted to tell his mother that his father had never cleaned guns in his study, and there was no one who went about that job more carefully. He wanted to tell her that he had seen the cartridges on the desk, and the blood on the wall, and that there was nothing left of his father's head. He had seen all that, he wanted to say, he understood it, and her story wasn't true. He wanted to tell her about their hunt in the morning, the meadows, the soil, the hills covered in bracken. But all that had happened, his thoughts, the colours

28

and smells, just existed side by side, unfinished, in a state of semi-consciousness. He couldn't yet connect them with each other.

Then his mother stood up and left the room.

6

Relations whom Sebastian didn't know came to the funeral. Some of them patted his head and asked whether he remembered them. An old lady with a mauve Alice band in her hair hugged him. Her dress smelled of mothballs.

The whole village had come. While the priest spoke beside the open grave, Sebastian went to stand beside his friend, who had also been obliged to wear a dark suit. His friend whispered that the raft was ready now, it was afloat again, even bigger than last year and much better. His friend asked when he would be coming back; they were only waiting for him.

That afternoon the family members sat in the garden of the house. The cook had baked sand cake, and the cream on top of it was running in the sun. At first the guests were awkward with each other, but soon they were all talking at once.

Sebastian's mother tapped a glass with a fork. The conversations died down, and everyone turned to her. She said how glad she was that so many of them had come to the funeral; it had done her good. She asked them for their understanding, she said, but she was going to sell the house. Her voice was steady. Then she sat down again.

There was still silence when his father's brother stood up. He swayed and propped his hands on the table, the tablecloth slipped, a cake-plate fell to the paving stones and broke. He had been drinking.

'My brother and I were born in this house – I love it and hate it, the house, the lake, the grounds. I both love and hate it all,' he said with a gesture of his hand. His voice was slurred. 'She's right. My brother and I thought we could begin the world all over again. But there's nothing you can begin again, nothing at all, everything's always there. He couldn't become what he wanted to be, and nor could I. I must, you see, I must . . . ' His wife was plucking his sleeve. 'Yes, yes,' he said, 'let me have my say.' But all the same he dropped back into his wicker chair. He picked up his glass. 'I drink to the end of it,' he said, and added, quietly, 'Thank God, my poor brother has it behind him now.'

Sebastian sat on the outside sill of a window, listening to his uncle. He didn't understand what he was talking about. His uncle could cut silhouettes out of paper and perform shadow-plays with them. He had married an Indian woman who was serious and strange. He had been living in Delhi for almost twenty years. Once they had all been on the island of Norderney together. His uncle had taken Sebastian out in a fishing boat very early in the morning. He had been drinking gin; Sebastian remembered him standing in the middle of the boat with the yellow gin bottle. His uncle had called Sebastian over to him, hugged him and shouted, 'The sea is so damn stupid.' Then he fell over. Later, the fishermen had carried him off the boat.

The night after the funeral, Sebastian got out of bed. He went down to the lake in his pyjamas and sat on the wooden landing stage. Maybe he could stay here in secret, he thought. There was a little room at the very back of the right wing of the house. The only access to it was through a built-in wardrobe; it would be ideal. Even the cook didn't know about it. He could hide there, his friend would bring him food, and when he was grown up he would get the house back again.

His father had said that the house would always be there, his parents and grandparents and all his ancestors had lived here, and Sebastian and his children and his grandchildren would live here too. You were lost without your home, he had said, even if keeping up such an old house as this was often a strain.

Sebastian thought of that, and he thought of his plan, and finally he went to sleep out there on the landing stage.

7

Two weeks after the funeral, Sebastian's mother set to work. She must 'wind up' the household, she said.

First an antiques dealer came from Munich, a man with sparse hair who wore a pair of purple-framed reading glasses hanging from a chain round his neck. He went round all the rooms with Sebastian's mother, stopping now and then to point at something. In the end he bought the silver cutlery, four eighteenth-century miniatures, three oil paintings in rather battered frames, the guns and the elephant tusks. He would have all those things collected, he said, making out a cheque.

A house clearance firm brought a skip and put it down outside the steps up to the front door. The firm's men spent a week carrying almost everything out of the house; the skip was changed twice a day. By midday the men already smelled of sweat; they wore only undershirts. Once they had settled into their surroundings they didn't always bring the things straight out to the skip. They put on the African masks, yelled gleefully and threw the spears at trees in the grounds.

Sebastian didn't understand what his mother was doing. She called it 'making a clean sweep'. His father's slides, his cine-films, even his notebooks went into the skip. She burned photographs and letters in a water butt in the garden. She had to 'clear up', she kept saying at this time, 'draw a line under it, put an end to it all.' He heard her going through the house, she called to him, but he didn't answer.

Sebastian sat on the steps up to the front door every day, in the shadow cast by the house, waiting for the cool of the evening. The walls beside the little flight of steps had sand-stone reliefs showing badgers, otters and beavers. His father always said you had only to stroke the nose of one of the otters as you left the house, and then you were sure to come home.

Just before the end of the holidays, a house agent came. The slogan on his car said 'We Bring Together the Wishes of Demanding People Worldwide'. The agent placed himself in front of the house, formed his hands into a tube like a tele-scope and said, 'Well, rather run-down, yes, but a lovely situation. We may be able to sell it.' He took a great many photographs. Later, Sebastian's mother and the agent sat out-side at the table under the chestnut trees. Sebastian heard his mother saying, 'As little as that?' and for a moment he thought she would keep the house after all.

*

On the day after the house agent's visit, Sebastian cycled out to the church for the first time since the funeral. He got off his bike at the cemetery gate and pushed it along the gravel path. He saw the gravestones of his ancestors, and read his own name on every one of them. At his father's grave he stopped. Someone had planted flowers; the metal watering can was still standing nearby. He knelt down and dug a hole with his hands. On top, the soil was warm from the sun, but as he dug deeper it became cold and damp. He had knocked the otter's nose off the sandstone façade of the wall with a hammer, and he laid it in the earth. 'You'd better come home now,' he said. 'I can't manage this on my own.'

At the end of the holidays his mother took him to Munich. She grumbled about the car, saying that it was too old, and that as soon as the house was sold she was going to buy a new one. She parked in the station forecourt. She was sorry, she said, but she couldn't go as far as the platform with him or she'd never get to the horse show in time. Sebastian got out, kissed her through the open window, and lifted his case from the back seat. She can't wave goodbye because of all the traffic, he thought as he watched her drive away.

He found the train, sat in his reserved seat and looked out of the window. Feeling in his pocket, he took his father's cigarette case out and ran his thumb over the jade stone in it. He thought of the wall behind the desk; it had already been repainted. As the train left the station, he placed the cigarette case on the folding table in front of him. The stone gleamed in the sun, its colour calm and regular. 'Imperial jade,' his father had once called it. The cigarette case dated from the twenties, and there were Japanese characters engraved inside it. Sebastian held the case up to his eyes. Sometimes the shadow of a tree or an electricity pylon fell on the jade stone, changing its colour.

He saw the house before him, the dark green of his childhood, the bright days. The colours smelled of the dust covering everything, they smelled like freshly mown grass in the afternoon and like thyme after rain, and like the reeds between the planks of the landing stage. He thought of the silk dresses that his mother once used to wear, he thought of her skin in the sun and the picture of the Arctic Ocean in his father's study. He didn't know what was real any longer, and he didn't know what was going to become of him.

8

Over the next few years at boarding school, Sebastian spent nearly all his time sitting in the library, reading. He went to India, the Sierra Nevada, into the jungle, he drove dog-sleighs and rode dragons, he caught whales, he was a seafarer, an adventurer, a traveller in time. He didn't distinguish between stories and reality.

The librarian noticed it first. He saw Sebastian talking excitedly to someone, although the boy was alone in the reading room. It struck the librarian as strange, and he reported it to the school management. The prefects and teachers discussed the incident, phone calls were made to Sebastian's mother, and finally it was decided to have the matter investigated.

The Holy Father in charge of his year's intake at the school went to the capital city with Sebastian. He said they were going to see a famous doctor who was a professor at the university.

The doctor was fat, he smelled of pea soup and he was already very old. But he didn't look like a medical doctor, and his consulting room didn't look like a medical doctor's surgery. African masks hung on its walls, and a chain made of bones lay on the desk. Sebastian and the Father went into the city to see the fat doctor five times. They were delightful excursions. After each visit, the Father always took Sebastian to a café, and he could choose whatever cake he liked.

On the last visit, the fat man said there was no need for Sebastian to come any more. He discussed something with the Father. Sebastian wanted to take note of it, but the men were using words that he didn't know. Visual hallucinations, said the fat man, and many other difficult terms.

Outside, Sebastian asked the Father what the fat doctor had said, because he was slightly afraid that he was ill. The Father reassured him: there was nothing much the matter, he said, it was just that he, Sebastian, imagined people and things that didn't exist. Children sometimes did that, he added, when the border between reality and what was in their heads wasn't perfectly clear yet. In time it would put itself right. The Father looked sad when he said that. Then they went into the café. Sebastian ordered a slice of marble cake, and the Father had a beer.

Sebastian didn't like to think that part of him had to be put right. The cook at home had a crooked finger, and said it had just grown that way. Sebastian did not want to have anything crooked and ugly in his head. He thought about it for a long time on the way back, and decided that it didn't matter if he went on talking to Odysseus, Hercules and Tom Sawyer. But he mustn't tell anyone; he must be more careful.

9

After Sebastian's mother had sold the house by the lake, she bought a modern equestrian centre near Freiburg. She lived there in a detached house with thin walls and a double garage.

There were twelve boxes in the stables; there was an indoor riding arena and a square paddock for dressage. A groom cleaned the way leading through the stables, the tack room and the inner courtyard every day; Sebastian's mother made a fuss if she spotted any cobwebs.

She rose at six every morning, and rode all her twelve horses until afternoon. From spring to autumn she went to horse shows at the weekends, and once reached the rank of national number two in dressage. She lived on the proceeds from the sale of the house by the lake and its woods.

Because of the long intervals between school holidays, Sebastian noticed the changes in her: her chin and nose grew more pointed, her mouth was thinner, veins stood out on her forearms.

When Sebastian visited her, he slept in a small room under the roof, where it was stuffy in summer and dark in winter. His mother used the room as her office when he wasn't occupying it. His own things, packed into two crates, were kept up in the attic.

In the holidays he went to horse shows with her. The show grounds were muddy, water collected in the ruts left by the motorized horseboxes, and the tents smelled of onions and burnt fat. In summer the horse droppings dried on the grass, heat turned people's faces red, and the air was full of the acrid smell of the horses' sweat. Men sat on folding chairs round the dressage paddock, watching their wives and daughters. They had a language of their own: a horse being ridden on the bit; they spoke of travers, flying changes, an extended trot. Sebastian realized that the women riders were addicted to their horses.

His mother didn't talk to him much; riding left her tired. She said she found her body a trial these days, the pain in her knees and her back and her hand. A doctor had warned her that the constant strain on the nerves of her throat meant they were wearing thin, and it would be dangerous to go on riding, too much of a risk. She tried giving it up for a week, and then got back on her horses. She had to ride, she said, there was no other option.

When Sebastian was sixteen his mother introduced him to her new boyfriend. He was in his mid-forties, half a head shorter than she was, with short grey hair, thick eyebrows and manicured fingernails. They met Sebastian at the station when he came home from boarding school.

They'd go and eat now, said the new boyfriend. He drove to a restaurant which he said was the best; his boss ate there, too. As the menu said, 'a former butcher's shop has been turned into the perfect replica of a French café of the turn of the century', and was now 'an authentic piece of France in the middle of Freiburg'. The tables were packed close together, there were too many customers in the room, the chairs were uncomfortable. It was very noisy. The new boyfriend shouted that the food here was excellent, and he addressed the waiter by his first name.

The new boyfriend looked at his watch and ordered for everyone. He knew what was good here, he said. While they waited for the food to come, he told Sebastian that he was a sales rep for plasterboard panels, in which there was 'a huge trade'. An article about him had once appeared in a local tabloid paper, when he had been doing all he could to get a Swedish car supplier to open an outlet in this city. The supplier had changed his mind before anything could come of it, but he himself was described as 'the fixer' in the newspaper story, and a name like that stuck, he said. He raised his eyebrows and spoke in a tone suggesting that it was a humorous idea, but Sebastian realized that he was proud of it. His mother said nothing, and seemed to have heard the story before.

'Everything has its price,' said the fixer. 'But if you can move your arse it makes no difference where you come from.'

The fixer put his hand on Sebastian's mother's thigh and looked down her neckline. The waiter brought a bottle of Clos de Beaujeu, although no one had ordered it. He could have a drink, the fixer told Sebastian, 'in honour of the day'. Sebastian asked for water.

Then the fixer shouted across the table at Sebastian, 'What are you planning to be?'

Sebastian shrugged. The fixer was playing with the salt shaker. He had fat fingers, although he wasn't fat otherwise. He wore a gold watch on a gold bracelet, with a magnifying section over the date on the face of the watch. Saliva was drying in the corners of the fixer's mouth. Sebastian imagined the fixer's mouth on his mother's.

'Don't you have any plans? Going to such an expensive school, and you don't have any plans?' asked the fixer.

Sebastian did not reply.

'What's that you have there?' asked the fixer. He reached into the pocket of Sebastian's coat, which was lying over the chair, and took out the book that Sebastian had been reading in the train.

'*Down the rivers of the windfall light*,' read the fixer slowly. 'What's this supposed to mean?' He laughed uproariously, holding the book aloft.

'It's a poem,' said Sebastian. He snatched the book from the fixer's hand, accidentally knocking a glass over. Wine soaked the tablecloth and ran on to the fixer's trousers. Sebastian apologized, saying he must get some fresh air.

He went outside. A homeless man was searching a rubbish bin at the bus stop. A very long, shiny car drove soundlessly past. The air weighed down on the street with a smell of asphalt and petrol. A woman walked by, shouting into a mobile phone, 'You've been a single long enough, that's what it is.' Sebastian smoked two cigarettes, one after the other and too fast. A photograph of the green fisherman's hut where Dylan Thomas had written the poems hung over his desk at the boarding school. He thought of it now.

When he returned to the restaurant, the 'Homemade Galloway Meatballs' that the fixer had ordered for him were cold.

*

The fixer drove home too fast. Sebastian felt the seat-belt cutting into his throat. The fixer and Sebastian's mother went to bed at once. Sebastian read from his book of poems for a little while longer, and then went out into the garden to smoke; his mother wouldn't have smoking in the house.

There was a light on in the bedroom. The fixer was standing beside the bed, naked, while Sebastian's mother slept. The fixer was holding a video camera in one hand, with the red diode blinking to show that filming was in progress. He was masturbating with the other hand. Sebastian could see himself reflected in the outside of the large panoramic window.

He went up to the room under the roof and sat at the Perspex desk in front of the window. He wanted to write a letter, but didn't know who to. He stared at the point of his pencil, and then got an Opinel knife with a wooden handle out of his case. He usually took it hiking with him. He cut off the top of his left forefinger, and watched the blood come out, dripping on the desk. For a moment he felt alive. Then he went into the bathroom and bandaged the wound.

Sebastian's mother and the fixer got married just under a year later. They celebrated the wedding in a castle hotel, known to the fixer from a reps' conference that was held there. The bridal couple went to the register office in a horse-drawn carriage, and Sebastian's mother wore a white dress. A marquee was erected outside the hotel, an entertainer with a Hammond organ was booked to provide music. The guests could dance only out there; the hotel manager had said the parquet flooring in the castle was too easily harmed.

The fixer had taken dancing lessons for the bridal waltz. All

45

the same, he stumbled and fell hard on the wooden floor. The music stopped for a moment, and a woman held her hand in front of her mouth. When the fixer stood up his trousers were covered with dust. The guests applauded, a man who had had too much to drink shouted that it was a good omen for the marriage, and everyone laughed.

Sebastian left the marquee. Then he heard his mother. She had linked arms with the fixer and brought him outside. They were quarrelling; the fixer shook his head and tore himself away.

The fixer went up to the illuminated castle, limping. A cat was asleep on the stone steps outside the entrance, moving its paws in its sleep. The fixer looked round. Then he kicked the cat in the stomach with the toe of his patent leather shoe.

10

Two years later Sebastian took his school-leaving certificate. The Father stood at the altar in the monastery church. He wished the students who were leaving luck. It was a long sermon; he preached it every year. He said the students had finished their schooldays and must now make their own mistakes. Their lives would begin today. He hoped that they would leave the world better than it was. After the sermon, students played two movements from the Trout Quintet.

Sebastian's mother had been unable to come, 'because of her nerves', she had said.

After Mass, Sebastian went to his room. In the last week before the leaving ceremonies, major industrial firms had set up their stands in the corridors of the boarding school. He had received offers from trainee programmes and courses leading to diplomas in applied sciences; a detergents manufacturer offered to finance his university studies. He sat at his desk. From here, he could see the Lukmanier Pass; he thought of his walks in the Rhine valley, and the wandering lights in the chestnut woods of the Val San Giacomo. He had been at

the boarding school for almost nine years. He took the indus-
trialists' business cards and threw them in the waste-paper
basket.

He went by train to Freiburg, where he caught the bus and then
carried his case home, almost a kilometre. He rang the doorbell. His mother's new dog barked. The light came on; he could
hear the fixer shouting at the dog. His mother opened the door.
She wore a blouse with a frilled collar. They hadn't been
expecting him until tomorrow, she said, she must have entered
it wrongly in her diary. Then she went back into her bedroom,
saying she wasn't well.

Sebastian made himself a sandwich in the kitchen. The fixer
sat at the table with him.

'What are you going to do now?' asked the fixer. 'You'll have
to do something. So what are your plans? How long do you
intend to stay here?'

'I'll tell you both in the morning,' said Sebastian.

'No, I want to know now. You've already woken me.' The
fixer had swollen eyes.

'It's been a long day; it really is too late,' said Sebastian. He
kept calm. He knew what was coming now.

The fixer jumped up, strode round the table and took up his
stance beside Sebastian's chair. The artery at his throat was pul-
sating. The last time the fixer hit him had been a year ago, when
Sebastian had wanted to visit his girlfriend from the girls'
boarding school in Italy, but the fixer had refused to let him go.
In a rage, he had dropped the fixer's car keys down a drain. The
fixer had hit him there in the street. Sebastian must learn dis-
cipline, he had said, he'd show him what was what, he had

shouted. Passersby had turned to look at them, and Sebastian's mother had stood there saying nothing.

Sebastian put the sandwich down on the plate. He stood up slowly. He was a head and a half taller than the fixer. He had spent an hour boxing every day at school for the last three years, he had played ice hockey and gone hill-walking in the mountains. His body was smooth and hard. He even wears that watch at night, thought Sebastian.

The fixer stared at Sebastian, apparently unsure what to do. Then he gave up. He dropped into a chair, he lost command of his features and his eyes turned dull.

Sebastian saw that his hair was very thin now. He took the plate, went to the door, and switched off the light behind him.

The next morning Sebastian got up early and went into the city. He bought some books, went to an exhibition and sat down in a café. He was waiting. When he returned to the house early in the afternoon, his mother was lying in a deckchair. The lawn had been mown short; she put nitrogen fertilizer on it every year. She was wearing sunglasses and the same blouse as yesterday, the edges of its frilled collar now brown with her foundation. She buttoned up her bathrobe and took off her sunglasses.

He looked at her and she looked at him.

Her feet were bare, their toes crippled by riding boots. The canvas of the deckchair was yellow and her legs were white and full of veins. He realized there was nothing more to say, because it was too long ago, and because there was no house by the lake any more, and no bright days. He would begin his life, and she would go on with hers. That was what they had decided, and now it was stupid to wonder whose fault it was.

He nodded to her, that was all he did. Then he closed the door to the terrace again, taking care to make no noise. He went up to the room under the roof. It was stuffy, so he opened the window. The wind blowing over the fields smelled of hyacinths and irises. He undressed and lay down on his bed. His muscles ached. He heard his mother walking up and down in the yard.

11

The photographer greeted Sebastian von Eschburg in a friendly manner. They had met at an old boys' reunion; the photographer had left Eschburg's boarding school with his own certificate thirty years earlier. He had studied at the Academy of Art in Düsseldorf, and in the eighties he had published pictorial albums, large black and white photos of coalmines, water towers, haulage plants and gasometers. Most of these features were no longer in existence. Eschburg liked the industrial images, no human beings in them, harsh photographs with a backdrop of pale grey skies.

The photographer was editor of a journal of architectural photography, a member of many committees, and chaired the jury panels for various competitions. He had written books about photography, he had a vast range of technical knowledge, and he regularly wrote reviews of photographic exhibitions in the major German newspapers. He made his living from photographs of residential and office buildings commissioned by architects and magazines. His photography was always immaculate, but he had never made an international name for himself. He claimed not to mind, but later Eschburg realized that it was a sore point.

In addition, the photographer ran four small studios in Berlin. They didn't bear his name, and he didn't do any photography for them himself. He called them his 'bread-and-butter business'. Passport and portrait photos were taken by the studios, wedding photographs, photos of birthday parties, the celebrations of business firms and graduating high school classes.

The photographer offered Eschburg a job working for him. Eschburg rented a small furnished room in Charlottenburg. At first the photographer paid him only a modest salary, but it was enough to live on. In those first months, Eschburg read the photographer's books and all the other works on photography that he could find. Systematically, he learned about lenses, lighting, apertures, filters, about shutter speeds in analogue and digital cameras, about large, medium and small formats. He developed pictures in the studio laboratory, he made notes on alkaline and acid baths, experimented with acetic and citric acid, with sodium and ammonium aluminium sulphate solutions. The photographer was a good teacher. They discussed the history of photography, they went to exhibitions and galleries together, and although the photographer was moody and could be unjust, Eschburg enjoyed his company.

To Eschburg, photography was far more than a trade. He worked only with black and white film, treating the prints later with thiocarbamide and sodium hydroxide. He experimented until his pictures had the soft, warm tone that took the harshness out of all the other colours in his head. The photographer told Eschburg that he must be revolutionary, art must be provocative and destructive, that this was the way to the truth. But Eschburg didn't want to be an artist. He wanted to create another world for himself with his photographs, a fluent and warm world of the past. And after a few months the subjects of his pictures, the human beings and the landscapes, looked the way he could tolerate them.

Eschburg often worked in the bread-and-butter studios, wanting to learn the daily business of their trade from the photographers employed there. Six months after he had begun working for the photographer, the owner of a perfumery came into one of these small studios. She wanted nude photographs of herself. She was in her mid-forties, and she and her husband had divorced a few months before; the pictures were to be for the new man in her life. She blushed when she said that.

Eschburg helped with the photographs. They were the usual kind of thing: the stretch marks of pregnancy veiled over with tulle, muted light to fade wrinkles out, filters to blur her buttocks, thighs and stomach, invisible strips of sticky tape lifting her breasts.

When the photographs were ready, Eschburg asked the woman if he could take a few pictures himself. She nodded. Eschburg used the second-hand Hasselblad that he had bought cheap. He liked the camera; the photographer doesn't see his model directly, and instead his view is diverted by means of a mirror. The result is less brutal. Eschburg put a film into the camera, opened the curtains of the studio and switched off the artificial light. He asked the woman to take off her makeup. It had been raining all day, and the light that afternoon was soft, a clear grey.

Eschburg talked to her, saying he had only just begun as a professional photographer, and was still unsure of himself. She relaxed. After an hour she was ready. Eschburg took twelve pictures very quickly, without using a tripod.

In the pictures, the woman was sitting on the bed with her knees drawn up, the lengths of fabric used in the other pictures lay on the floor, and she was looking out through the window. A rectangle of light was shed on the sheet and her face. Her body was pallid, only her forehead brighter – a woman of forty-six with her dignity wounded.

Two days later the woman came to collect the pictures for her boyfriend, slipping them quickly into her bag. Eschburg also showed her the photographs that he had taken, telling her he wasn't charging for those. She stood there looking at the pictures one by one, then turned them over, tore them up and placed them on the counter. Still standing in front of Eschburg, she opened her mouth, but no words came out.

The photographer changed as the years went on; he lost his ability to concentrate, ate too much and put on more and more weight. When he forgot delivery deadlines he shouted at his employees and slammed doors. Next day he would be sorry, and in that mood he used to say his life had run through his fingers. He had three daughters who wanted nothing to do with his work. He had stayed with his wife for the sake of comfort and fear of loneliness. Sometimes Eschburg thought the photographer saw him as the son that he had never had.

*

Eschburg could almost always salvage the photographer's deadlines, working through the night and delivering the pictures punctually. When he told the photographer, after four years, that he must move on now and try something else, the photographer was furious. He had made him great, said the photographer, he had taught Eschburg all he knew; but for him, the photographer, he would be nothing. The photographer's face was red and his mouth very thin as he said it.

That afternoon Eschburg went back early to the furnished room where he was still living. He sat at the window and watched the passersby in the street. He thought of the photographer's large pictures and the truth that they showed. The pictures would long outlast the photographer who had taken them. He had not wasted his life; as a young man he had been very good, and in his old age he was still better than most others.

Eschburg wrote the photographer a long letter. He sat at his desk for many hours, but in the end he tore the letter up and threw it away.

12

Eschburg rented a two-storey factory building in the yard of a house in Berlin-Mitte. The factory used to make umbrellas, but the building had been standing empty since German reunification. It had tall windows, the walls were reddish-yellow brick, and it was not expensive.

He set up his studio on the lower floor, and moved into the living quarters on half of the upper floor with his private possessions. As he was carrying his cartons of books up, he met his neighbour for the first time; her apartment occupied the other half of that floor. They introduced themselves to each other in the corridor.

Eschburg called all the editors and architects he knew, saying he had set up on his own. Gradually commissions came in, photographs for sales catalogues, small illustrated news stories about new buildings, sometimes photos for one of the city's museums. He had spent very little money while he was working for the photographer, he didn't need much, and he enjoyed his independence.

There was an old armchair in his apartment; someone had put it out on the street to be taken away with the rubbish. Its black upholstery had worn thin, but it was still comfortable. Apart from that, he had nothing but two iron chairs, a rough-hewn wooden table, shelves for his books and a bed.

The editor of a cinema magazine asked Eschburg to take a photograph of a well-known actress for an article. She arrived wearing no makeup, warm from riding her bicycle to his studio, and wearing a plain white shirt. He photographed her just as she was; it took him hardly a quarter of an hour.

Eschburg was in luck. The actress was pleased with the photo and put it on her website. She recommended Eschburg to her colleagues and friends. Soon he was taking photographs of directors, actors, sports stars and singers. Then came the politicians, managers and entrepreneurs. Eschburg made a name for himself because the people he photographed were well known. Three years later he had published two volumes of photographs. He had taken hundreds of black and white portrait photos, there were exhibitions of his work in various cities, his pictures featured on music CDs, on posters and in magazines, and they hung in restaurants. He could charge high prices for his work. Eschburg was only twenty-five years old.

His world changed. It took him an hour every day to answer his emails, and two hours to organize his engagements diary. An agency looked after the exploitation of rights to his pictures, another agency took care of his website. He had an advertising contract with a camera manufacturer. He travelled a great deal, and often woke up in hotels not knowing what city he was in. Sometimes that made him think it would be better to lie in bed and wait until all this was over.

13

Four years after Eschburg's move to Linienstrasse, a woman called his studio and asked if he had time to see her. She was quite close, she said, and would like to look in. She gave the name of a French energy company to which she was adviser. Half an hour later she rang his doorbell. She was wearing a thin yellow dress and had pinned her hair up on top of her head.

'Just call me Sofia, my surname's far too complicated.' Her hand was warm. Her business card told him that she was managing director of a public relations firm. She said that the energy company she was advising wanted to launch an advertising campaign with the face of a woman, and asked whether he would care to take the photographs for it.

'How did you find me?' asked Eschburg.

She smiled. 'Not by way of your famous portraits. Years ago I saw one of your photos in the office of your former employer. You weren't there yourself that day. It was hanging in your office. A small black and white photo of a woman.'

Eschburg had kept the pictures of the naked woman that he

took in the photographer's bread-and-butter studio. One of them hung over the desk where he worked.

'Yes, that's the one I mean,' she said, pointing to the picture. She went over to the desk and looked at it. Eschburg stationed himself beside her. Sofia leaned forward; the nape of her neck was slim.

'I like that picture; it's honest. Just the kind of thing we could use in the campaign,' said Sofia. She turned to him too quickly, so that their faces almost touched. They stood like that for a moment.

'Show me some more of your photos, would you?' she said.

Eschburg placed the pictures that he had taken over the last few years on the desk. She picked up each in turn. Sometimes she said, 'That's good.' She sounded very sure of her judgement.

'Would you like a coffee?' he asked.

She shook her head; she was concentrating so intently that she seemed to perceive nothing else. After half an hour she had made a selection.

'Can I take these photos with me? You'll get them back,' she said. Light fell on her face through the high windows.

'May I take a photograph of you?' asked Eschburg.

She laughed. 'I'd have to put something else on. I look terrible.'

'No, please don't; we can do it now. It will be good, you'll see.'

He brought the 10 x 15 centimetre baseboard camera down from his apartment; its casing was made of wood, and he had bought it in a flea market years ago. Sometimes he took photos with it; he liked its weight, the complicated mechanism, the elaborate development of the photos in the darkroom. He had converted the camera to use modern flat film.

'You mustn't move,' he said as he screwed the camera to the tripod and prepared the cassette. 'Only a second. This camera has no depth of focus; if you move the picture will be lost.'

Sofia stood in front of the back wall of the studio. Suddenly she pulled the zip fastener of her dress down and let it slip to the floor. She kicked it off and stood naked in front of the bare bricks of the wall. Although she was in her mid-thirties, she had the body of a young girl. She folded her hands behind her back.

When he had taken the picture she said that she would like something to drink now. He went to get a bottle of water out of the fridge. When he came back, she had dressed again. She closed her eyes as she drank, swallowed the wrong way, and water ran down her throat. She wiped her mouth with the back of her hand.

Half an hour later she went away, leaving the agreement for the energy company's photographs and her business card lying on the desk. She had written her mobile number on the back of the card.

There had been many women in Eschburg's life during the last few years. Women liked him, and he never had a particularly difficult time. He slept with them, but that never really moved him. Usually he couldn't even remember their names a few days later. If he happened to meet them again he was courteous, but was not to be pinned down. Twice he had thought he was fond of a woman, but the feeling had worn off a week later.

That night he developed the picture of Sofia. He enlarged but did not retouch it. He hung the print on a wall in the studio. The background was blurred and dark, a strand of hair fell over her forehead, her face was pale and intent.

Her arms were outside the picture; she was only a torso.

14

Sofia called Eschburg a few days later. She said she would be spending the weekend in Paris, where her agency was organizing a dinner. He really must come; the electricity company would pay for everything. Eschburg packed his travelling bag, and placed her photo on top of his shirts.

When he came out of the arrivals hall at Charles de Gaulle airport, he couldn't see her. He stood outside the automatic doors. Men and women on business were hurrying out. Someone pulled a wheelie case over his foot, and a child's scream rang through the hall.

Eschburg sat down on a metal bench. He opened his bag and looked at the photo.

'It came out well,' she said. He hadn't noticed her sitting down beside him. She kissed him on the cheek.

She had hired a car. Paris was unbearable in summer, she said, but the seaside resort of Deauville was wonderful at this time of year. The dinner given by her agency was not, in fact, for another two days.

She drove the little car too fast, phoning her clients on the way. She had two phones; she spoke French, English, Arabic and German. He looked out of the window. A point came when he stopped listening to her. This was a mistake, he thought, and he couldn't now think why he was sitting in a car beside this woman.

Sofia wanted to drive along the coastal road. Thirty kilometres from Deauville it began raining so hard that they had to stop. Sofia parked the car under a tree. She bent down to him, kissed him, and opened his trousers. He had an almost painful erection. She sat on top of him. Through the rear window, he saw a cyclist who had taken shelter under the same tree. The man's hair was hanging over his face; he stared at Eschburg and Sofia. Eschburg closed his eyes. Sofia was lying on him now, her face close to his. Her movements, her aroma were strange to him. The car windows were steaming up. After half an hour the rain slackened, and they drove on.

All the Deauville hotels were fully booked, but they found a room in a run-down boarding house. They went down to the sea, and sat on a bench in the drizzling rain, not touching.

Long after they had fallen asleep in the boarding house, he woke and went out on the tiny balcony, closing the door behind him. The sky was black and merged with the sea. It would soon start raining again. The neon advertisement on the boarding house shone on the wall above him. He wondered whether there would be a train back to Paris at this time of night; he could go down to the station now and find out. He went back into the room, looked for his clothes in the dim light and put them on.

'Don't go,' she said.

'It's too complicated,' he replied. He had his shoes in his hand.

'It always is,' she said. 'Come here.'

He lay down on the bed beside her fully dressed. He looked at the dust on the slats of the wooden Venetian blinds. Sofia's breath was calm and steady. He gradually relaxed.

She turned over on her stomach and propped her chin in her hands. 'Are you always so serious?'

'I don't know,' he said.

'Your photos are serious. You're doing something that I don't yet understand with those pictures. My father was like that, but he died long ago,' she said. 'Did you know that the colour of your photographs, that sepia colour, is the ink of the squid? Many doctors prescribe it for depression, to cure lone-liness and a sense of the void. They say it can heal a human being's wounded dignity.'

He heard the wind and the rain, which had begun to fall again and was beating against the window panes.

'What about your parents?' she asked.

'I'm not in touch with my mother any more.' His mouth was dry.

'And your father?'

He did not reply. He thought of the house by the lake, far away now, and then he was glad of Sofia's voice, her mouth, her hair and her skin that was warm and the colour of bronze.

'Did seeing that cyclist arouse you?' she asked after a while.

'You noticed him?' he asked.

She nodded. Then she stood up and opened the door out into the corridor. She came back to bed, pushed up his shirt and unzipped his trousers. She kissed his chest and belly, and slipped between his legs. He wanted to pull her down to him, but she pressed him back on the bed. He felt her breasts on his thighs. She pushed her hair away from her face so that he could see her.

He wondered whether all this meant anything, if the room meant anything, or the picture over the sofa, or the balcony with its iron railing. It must mean something, but he didn't know what.

It took him a long time to reach climax.

As soon as it was lighter outside, he got up and fetched croissants and coffee from the breakfast room. Sofia had gone back to sleep with her mouth open; she looked like a child. He sat on the balcony with his coffee. The beach was dark with rain.

15

Two weeks later, the model for the advertising campaign was sitting on a stool in front of the brick wall in Eschburg's studio. It was going to be a good photograph, like all the photos he took. Eschburg looked through the viewfinder. He didn't know how often he had taken this picture already. The woman's head and breasts were thrust forward, her throat was taut, she was smiling. Her face was perfectly symmetrical. The links of her necklace will be visible in the picture as an oval, they'll have the brightness of her teeth, Eschburg thought. He saw it all even before he pressed the shutter. It felt wrong to take the picture. He could no longer distinguish between the people in front of the camera.

'I'm sorry,' he said quietly to the woman. 'You're very pretty, but I can't photograph you.'

The model stayed sitting where she was. She looked at the manager of the advertising agency, and then stopped smiling. The manager began talking, his voice rose, he said something about payment and deadlines, he threatened damages and lawyers. Eschburg carefully put the camera back in its wooden case.

That afternoon he went to the Old National Gallery. The picture he had come to see hung on the second floor. It was smaller than he remembered it, 1.70 metres wide, with a label beside it: *Caspar David Friedrich*, Monk By The Sea, *1810*. The painter had never signed it, nor given it a date or a title. The construction was simple: sky, sea, rock. Nothing else, no houses, no trees, no bushes. Nothing but a tiny figure standing left of centre, with its back to the viewer, the only vertical in the composition. Friedrich had worked on it for two years; he had been suffering from depression while he painted it.

The picture was first exhibited in 1810. Heinrich von Kleist wrote, at the time, that in looking at it you felt as if your eyelids had been cut away.

16

Sofia and Eschburg were spending every weekend together now. Eschburg told her that he couldn't go on taking those photographs. She suggested a visit to Madrid; there was something she wanted to show him there, she said. At the airport, they took a taxi to the museum. Sofia had spent time here once; she showed Eschburg the buildings where she had lived, she mentioned names he didn't know, squares, cafés, her voice low and quiet. She told him that she had been in love with an older man at the time. Their relationship had lasted three years, and then he went back to his wife and children. She herself had moved to Paris to begin a new life.

They went into the Prado through the visitors' *Goya* entrance, crossed the halls of Italian and Flemish painting, passed pictures by Titian, Tintoretto and Rubens, making straight for Goya's picture of the royal family. To the right, in Room 36, hung the two pictures numbered 72. Both showed the same young woman lying on a sofa. In the left-hand picture she was clothed, in the right-hand picture naked. Seen from any angle, the tip of the clothed Maja's shoe pointed at the observer.

School students were sitting in a semi-circle on the floor in front of their teacher. Some of the girls were already wearing lipstick. The teacher asked her students to describe the differences between the two paintings. Sofia interpreted for him. One girl said that the clothed Maja in the picture was blushing because she was ashamed, but the naked Maja was pale and did not look at anyone. She didn't understand that, said the student, surely it ought to be the other way around? The teacher explained that Goya had painted the two pictures, *The Naked Maja* and *The Clothed Maja*, for the prime minister of Spain. They had been linked by a folding mechanism that allowed you to see either one or the other version, either the naked or the clothed woman. The minister had hung them in his 'Erotic Cabinet' of works of art. At a later date, the Inquisition had the two paintings locked away.

The girl asked what an erotic cabinet was, and her teacher tried to explain. She said that *The Naked Maja* had been the first Spanish picture to show a woman's pubic hair. One of the boys dug the boy next to him in the ribs and grinned. The teacher said something that Sofia didn't understand to the boys, whereupon the first boy grinned even more and went red in the face, and one of the lipstick-wearing girls told him he was still a baby. The teacher stood up and led her students into the next hall.

For a moment Sofia and Eschburg were left alone with the pictures. Sofia said that before that painting of the Maja, artists had portrayed naked women only as angels, nymphs, goddesses, or in historical scenes. Men could look at such images without feeling ashamed. 'The Maja is different. She has large breasts, a narrow waist, lips painted red. She knows how beautiful she is, and she knows what she's doing,' said Sofia.

Eschburg thought of the other man with whom Sofia had slept in this city. He thought of that other man touching her body, her skin under the summer dress, and the pale scar above the left eyebrow.

'Goya was exposing the men of his time with that picture, if you see what I mean, Sebastian: they were staring at a naked woman, not an angel or a goddess. They had no excuses left. It was those men, not the Maja, who were shown naked,' said Sofia.

The wording on a panel beside the pictures told visitors, in both Spanish and English, that it was not certain whether the Maja was the Duchess of Alba or some other woman.

'Who was the Duchess of Alba?' asked Eschburg.

'Probably Goya's lover,' Sofia told him. 'Goya spent a summer on her estate after her husband had died. He painted a picture for her – it was a declaration of love. The duchess, all in black, is pointing to the ground, where lettering in the sand says *solo Goya*, "Goya alone". But of course solo also means "only". The duchess's lover was "only Goya", only the painter, a nobody. Many people do think that this duchess modelled for the Maja. Maybe they're right, or then again maybe not.'

They stayed standing in the small room in front of the two pictures for some time longer. It was warm. Sofia stood beside him, living and breathing and, here, belonging entirely to him. And then he felt afraid of losing her, because of the way he was.

'Yes, the Maja is the right picture,' he said.

*

Later, they went into every antiques dealer's shop they passed. At last she found what she was looking for: an old tin cigar box with a reproduction of the naked Maja on its lid. The colours were faded. She said these little tins used to be very common, and the cigars they contained were a brand known as 'Goya'. The antiques dealer said they were still made on the Canary Islands.

Out in the street again, Sofia took his arm.

'Do you like children?' she asked suddenly. She put the question as if that were all it was, just a question.

Eschburg didn't look at her.

An old woman was pushing a shopping trolley along the pavement; it was rusty, one wheel was faulty and she couldn't keep the trolley going straight. It was full of bags, plastic and fabric bags. All the old lady's possessions, thought Eschburg.

He put an arm round Sofia and drew her close. He was going to answer her, but she turned to him and shook her head.

'That was too soon,' she said, and kissed him.

He felt awkward and stupid.

The old woman with the shopping trolley stopped. She spat on the ground.

Eschburg searched his pocket for cigarettes. Sofia said she was hungry. They went to a restaurant that she knew in the Calle Toledo. Pictures of Spanish film stars hung on the first floor. They ate green peppers in hot olive oil, with coarse sea salt.

In their hotel, the dry heat of the city came in through the open windows.

'You're never entirely with me,' she said. 'There's always only part of you here, while another part is somewhere else.'

They had undressed, and were lying on the bed.

'I like it that you're different, but I often think part of you is missing. You're not in a good way,' she said.

'You must help me,' he replied.

'What with?' she asked.

'Everything,' he said, not knowing what else to say.

He couldn't explain that he thought in images and colours, not in words. He couldn't tell her about the gunshot in the house by the lake, or the knife cutting into the belly of the deer. Not yet.

'What are you looking for, Sebastian? Can you tell me?' she asked.

He shook his head. No one can understand another person, he reflected.

'You're difficult to live with,' she said wearily.

Suddenly he felt sure that it would be all right with her. A time would come when she did understand it all: the mists, the void, the deafness. Next moment he wanted to be alone, waiting until things rearranged themselves and calmed down.

They heard the tourists in the square outside the hotel. She was lying on his arm, which had gone to sleep, but Eschburg didn't trust himself to move. He felt her skin on his, and thought of the colour of hollyhocks. She was full of life, and he was a stranger to himself. He no longer knew whether what he was seeing was real.

All he knew was that he would hurt her.

17

Sofia and Eschburg had lost their way and arrived a quarter of an hour late. The description of the route to take wasn't particularly complicated, but there were no signposted roads there any more, only footpaths and forest tracks. They were close to the old house by the lake.

The house they were visiting was small and square. It was right at the top of a hill, surrounded by forest, and the trees were taller than the house.

The man had been waiting for them. He came down the steps past shrubs and bushes. He was wearing a black leather jacket and black-framed sunglasses, none of which suited the house. He was a porn producer, and looked the part. But when he took his sunglasses off, he was just an old man with grey eyes.

As they climbed the steps to the house, the porn producer said that in winter you could get there only with snow chains on your tyres or in a Unimog, and his nearest neighbour was fifteen kilometres away. He showed Sofia and Eschburg into the living room, where they sat down on the sofa. The porn producer went into the kitchen to make coffee. The house had low ceilings and smelled of damp earth. Photographs of exotic birds, sandwiched between unframed sheets of glass, hung on the living room walls. Under the photos were captions: 'Japurá, 6.35 hours', 'Mantaro, 20.49 hours', 'Juruá, 14.17 hours', and so forth. After a while the porn producer came back with a tray. The cups were thin and clinked against each other. Eschburg wondered on what principle the photos were arranged.

'I don't understand why you want to get these photographs taken,' said the porn producer, once he was installed in the only armchair. 'I don't think you'll like my studio. Twenty years ago things were different, but there are no screenplays for these films nowadays. One of my scriptwriters has switched to television and is writing serial hospital dramas. Anyone can make a film today. Every housewife who needs money for the rent has her own website and camera. If you want to survive as a producer you have to specialize.'

The porn producer had large hands. He never put them on the table, as if he were ashamed of them. He himself directed all the films he produced, he said.

He had bought an almond cake and a raspberry cake in the village. The raspberry cake was very good, he told Sofia, she really must try it.

'I've had to specialize, there was no alternative. I shoot films with large casts now. It's not so easy for amateurs to imitate those.'

*

Eschburg and Sofia had watched two of his films. Each of them featured only one woman, a young woman. The women didn't seem to be professional actors; they were more like students or trainees. First the porn producer interviewed the young woman in front of the camera. He talked to her perfectly normally, as you would when meeting someone socially. He asked how old she was, where she came from, what her interests were. While he was talking to her, men joined them. The camera focused only on their pricks. The men spurted their sperm into the woman's face as she went on talking about ordinary, everyday subjects. She was not allowed to wipe the sperm off. After the interview with the porn producer the camera moved back, and then the woman had to fellate other men, twenty-five or thirty of them. She had at most a minute to bring each of them to climax. After all the men had sprayed their sperm onto her face, the camera accompanied the woman to the bathroom. While she was washing herself, the porn producer interviewed her again. Then he asked how she had felt about it.

The porn producer ate a piece of the raspberry cake. 'A film like that is made up of many small details,' he said. 'I've experimented with the setting as well; these days I use only black walls and floors.'

Sofia told the porn producer what Eschburg's pictures would look like, and what changes they would have to make in the studio. She laid some drawings out on the table. The porn producer looked hard at everything, and asked questions about details. When they were discussing money, Eschburg asked how he was to pay the men.

'I don't pay them anything,' said the porn producer. 'They're amateurs. They just have to have an up-to-date HIV test; I insist on that to protect the women. And they have to shave their genitals, but those are the only conditions. I always get more volunteers than I need. If you want to pay them, that's your business, but it won't cost you much.'

The porn producer's most successful film was called *Venus In Her Bath Of Sperm*. He had won the Erotic Film Industry's prize for it, roughly equivalent to a platinum disc in the world of music.

The porn producer drank his coffee. He had been talking a great deal, and now looked wearier than ever. Suddenly it was very quiet. Eschburg looked out of the window. There was a pile of freshly cut firewood outside the house, the billets of wood neatly stacked above each other; they would be dry by next winter. Beyond the firewood was the lawn, and beyond that the forest began.

Eschburg thought of Botticelli's painting, *The Birth of Venus*. Kronos cuts off the genitals of his father Uranus and throws them into the sea behind him. The blood and sperm make the sea foam and give birth to Venus. Botticelli painted her face as grave and lovely; in his depiction, she remains remote from such things. She understands, she feels regret, but she never becomes a part of that world.

'I'd rather make other films,' said the porn producer, breaking the silence. 'I've thought of making a documentary about the flight of migratory birds to Africa. Did you know that many birds fly five thousand kilometres to the warmer countries? They really do. They sense the angle of inclination of the earth's magnetic field. But fewer and fewer birds have been flying south in the last few years. It's because of climate change. The warm Gulf Stream and the cold Humboldt Current are being diverted.'

The porn producer's voice was softer now.

'I suspect,' he said, 'that the migratory system may soon come to an end. Even today, starlings are overwintering in European cities. Perhaps I'll make that film yet some day.'

They sat in the living room for a little longer. The porn producer told them about his daughter who wanted to study archaeology. Then he suddenly got to his feet, went to the door without a word, and put his leather jacket on again. There was a splinter left from his wood-cutting on its woollen collar. He took Sofia and Eschburg back to their car, and said they could come back any time they liked. He shot a film every week.

They drove back through the forest. It was cooler now, and the trees were reflected in the painted finish of the car bonnet. Eschburg said that the birds on the walls had been arranged by colour, not by the tributaries of the Amazon. Sofia had tears in her eyes.

He wanted to show her the old house beside the lake. The village had changed: the pharmacist had gone, to be replaced by two street cafés and a modern metal fountain. The street had been given a new layer of asphalt. The crooked box hedge and the drive up to the house had gone as well. There was now a car park, full of expensive-looking cars with number plates from Munich and Starnberg. Wooden holiday chalets stood in the park. They were painted white, had verandas overlooking the lake, and were all the same size.

The old house had been renovated and re-roofed, and the first-floor windows had been enlarged. There was a notice beside the flight of steps up to the entrance: 'Golf Club members only.'

They went down to the lake. The landing stage, the boathouse and the stables had been torn down, and golf buggies were left in what had been the chapel. There were new white gravel paths between the holiday chalets, and new flowerbeds, and weatherproof plastic benches stood on the grass. A new teak terrace stood behind the house, with people sitting on it under sun umbrellas, wearing yellow and red tank tops and check trousers and skirts.

'I'm so sorry,' said Sofia.

Eschburg wanted to tell her about the rusty weathervane on the roof. He wanted to tell her that the colours here had been bronze, lemon and cadmium yellow, cyan blue, olive and chromium oxide green, burnt sienna and sand. He wanted to tell her that reality moved faster than he did, that he couldn't keep up. Things passed on, and he was only watching.

All he actually said was, 'That's where the boathouse used to stand.'

A man in a blue jacket came over the grass. 'Excuse me, please, are you members?' he asked. He was young and polite, and he had very white teeth.

'No,' said Eschburg.

'Then I'm afraid I must ask you to leave the club premises.'

Only the lake hadn't changed. The reeds were still there, and the dark green trees, and the pollen drifting on the water.

'I understand,' said Eschburg.

*

On the way to the airport they stopped at a fuel station. While Eschburg was waiting for Sofia after paying, he leafed through the newspapers and magazines on the shelves above the sweets and crisps. The headline of one tabloid announced that mankind was bankrupt, was fifty trillion euros in debt. In debt to whom, Eschburg wondered. He bought cigarettes and a new plastic lighter. On the way to the car he felt sick. He threw up between the petrol pumps.

A few hours later they were back on the plane to Berlin. She's the first woman I can imagine being with, he thought. I can be alone and silent with her. He put his hand on hers and held it tightly.

Sofia looked at him as if he were a stranger.

From above, they could see the neat and tidy fields, geometrically marked out strips, squares of maize and clover. The tidiness soothed Eschburg.

18

Eschburg worked on the pictures for two months. He entitled them *The Maja's Men*. Sofia was shown lying on a sofa copied by a set designer from the one in Goya's paintings. In the first picture Sofia was naked. Sixteen men in suits were standing round her, staring at her. Sofia lay in the same position as Goya's Maja, and was made up in the same way. The camera also saw her from Goya's viewpoint.

In the second picture, Sofia was dressed like *The Clothed Maja*. The men stood in exactly the same way as in the first picture, but now they were naked. They stared at Sofia with their heads in the same attitude as before, their pricks were erect, and pointing to Sofia's face and body. Two of the men had sprayed their sperm on her blouse.

The men were the amateurs used by the porn producer for his films. They were of different sizes; several had paunches, one had a plaster on his forearm, five were bearded, four wore glasses. The camera showed every slight reddening of their skin and every hair in ultra-sharp dimensions.

Eschburg had taken the photographs in the porn producer's

studio, using a Hasselblad 503 CW and a 39 megapixels digital scan back. They had been exposed by Grieger in Düsseldorf on a LightJet 500 XL in the 1.80 x 3.00 metre format, and printed on acrylic plates.

The two plates hung one behind the other. At first you saw only the photograph of Sofia naked and the men clothed. Then, at two-minute intervals, an electric motor pushed the front plate up over hinges, to reveal the picture with Sofia clothed and the men naked. After that the first photo slid back to its original position.

When the electric motor had been installed, Eschburg climbed up the external metal staircase to the roof of the factory building. That first summer after moving into Linienstrasse four years earlier, he had sometimes spent the night up there. The two chestnut trees in the yard reminded him of home. Later, he often wondered why he had climbed to the roof that day. Perhaps it was the heat, or weariness, or something else for which he had no explanation.

A woman was lying on the Hollywood swing seat that had always stood on the roof. She was wearing espadrilles and a silk kimono that looked old and grubby. Eschburg was about to go away again.

'You're welcome to stay,' said the woman.

The tar on the roof was soft from the heat. The woman had a pale scar on her forehead.

'We met a few years ago when I was moving in,' said Eschburg.

'Senja Finks,' the woman introduced herself. 'I won't shake hands; it's too hot.'

She was in her mid-thirties. She had a scarf over her hair and was wearing large-framed sunglasses. She looked rather unkempt.

'Sit down,' she said.

The upholstery of the swing was stained and torn, with yellow foam stuffing coming out of it.

'Would you like a beer?' asked Senja Finks. 'It's chilled.'

'Do you have anything else?'

'Only beer.'

'Then yes, I'll have one,' said Eschburg.

Senja Finks opened a coolbox, took out a bottle and opened it with a plastic cigarette lighter. The swing moved slowly back and forth. Her perfume smelled of cedars and earth.

'You take photographs, don't you?' asked Senja Finks.

'Yes,' said Eschburg.

She took another beer out of the coolbox for herself. As she opened it, it foamed over on the kimono, her bare knee and the rooftop. The foam was quick to dry on the hot roof, leaving a white outline.

'Where are you from?' asked Eschburg, feeling that he ought to ask some kind of question. 'I mean, what is your accent?'

'I'm from Odessa on the Black Sea. I've been here for over ten years.' She wiped her mouth with the back of her hand.

'And what do you do?' asked Eschburg.

'Nothing,' she said. After a while she added, 'I've done everything already.'

Eschburg considered that last remark, and no longer felt awkward about remaining silent. They drank the beer; Senja Finks rolled herself cigarettes of dark tobacco and smoked. After a while Eschburg nodded off to sleep.

When he woke up again, he didn't know how much time had passed. He said he must go now. His knee hit the iron table, and a bottle half full of beer tipped over. Senja Finks was so quick that Eschburg didn't see her movement. It was an automatic reaction, unconscious, precise, sure. She caught the bottle with her left hand before it could smash on the rooftop below them. She was breathing no faster than before.

Her kimono had fallen open. Her stomach was flat and hard. Eschburg saw the scars all over her torso, long weals as if they had been left by a whip. There was an owl under her left breast. At first he thought it was a tattoo; then he realized that someone had branded it on her skin with a hot iron.

19

The exhibition of *The Maja's Men* was a success. A TV cultural magazine programme had transmitted a preview, and on the afternoon of the opening there was a long line of people waiting outside the gallery.

Sofia was wearing a black dress and had tied her hair back. She was slim and elegant as she moved among the guests, distributing business cards, laughing one moment and the next moment serious again.

He thought of the ladder in her tights that had been bothering her before the exhibition, and how she had gazed out of the kitchen window that morning without saying anything. She had been watching a little boy playing in the yard. Then she had turned to him, and he had seen the question that she no longer asked and that he could not answer.

Eschburg looked at Sofia. All this is possible only with her, he thought, the photographs, and still being with her, and enduring.

Eschburg left the viewing, went back to Linienstrasse, packed a few things and went to the Charlottenburg municipal swimming pool. It had been built in 1898, three storeys high, a red brick building with a Jugendstil façade, its roof a structure of steel girders like a market hall.

He went through the green iron door. At this time of day he was almost always alone here. He changed, showered, and let himself down the steps and into the pool. He swam a few lengths, fast and steadily. Then he turned on his back and looked up at the sky through the high glass ceiling. He breathed out and dropped to the bottom of the pool, where he stayed underwater until it hurt. The samurai of ancient Japan used to rise every morning saying, 'You are dead.' It made the idea of death easier. He thought of that now, and was at ease.

Eschburg returned to his studio. There were prostitutes in high-heeled shoes standing in Oranienburgerstrasse; their wigs were very blonde or very black, and sweat left narrow runnels in their makeup.

There was still a queue waiting outside the gallery. Eschburg carried on until he came to an art-house cinema, where he bought a ticket for the film that had just begun. He sat at the end of the back row. The sound in the cinema was loud, and the cutting of the film too fast; he couldn't make out what was happening.

After half an hour he left the cinema again. It was hardly any cooler. The pavements were full of people, buskers playing music outside a café, a few drunken tourists dancing.

He walked the streets until he was tired. He stopped at a building site. It smelled of drains and shit. Eschburg looked down, and saw a fox lying among the pipes, its coat wet and full of sand. He stared at the dead fox, and then he thought the fox was staring back at him.

20

When Eschburg came into the studio next morning, Sofia was
already at her desk.

'*The Maja's Men* was sold yesterday,' she said. 'To a Japanese.
You're rich.' She laughed.

The iron hooks that had held it were still in the studio wall.

'It would never have happened but for you,' he said.

She looked happy and tired.

'Shall we go away?' he said. 'We could rent a house on
Mallorca.'

'Yes,' she said.

They had hardly slept for the last few nights before the exhibition. Sofia sat at the computer to search for holiday houses.
Early the next day they flew out.

They hired a car at the airport, and drove down the highway
to Santanyí in the south-east of the island. The air condi-
tioning wasn't working; Sofia tied a scarf over her hair and let
the window down. The air was hot and salt. They stopped in
Llucmajor.

The espresso in the Café Colon was burnt, market women

were talking loudly at the bar, the fruit machine was on. They bought a few things in a food store and climbed back into the car. Beyond S'Alqueria Blanca they turned off the main road and drove between narrow walls up to the house.

That evening they toasted dark bread and ate it with olive oil, tomatoes and garlic. The sea was almost two kilometres away, but even up here it smelled of seaweed. They sat on the terrace, where they could see over the almond trees and Aleppo pines down to the plain and on to the sea. The earth was red with iron oxide.

He was woken by the misfiring of a motorbike somewhere down on the road. Sofia was no longer lying beside him. He went into the garden. She was sitting in a deckchair near the pool.

'Perhaps these are our last days,' she said.

He looked at her. The underwater lighting from the pool was greenish-blue.

'What do you mean?' He was awake but at the same time felt dull-witted. He wanted to go back to bed.

'I'm afraid you won't be here any more. And I'm afraid of your fantasies. Loving you is such a strain.' She was silent, and so was Eschburg. Then she said, 'Who are you, Sebastian?'

Eschburg got up and went to find a bottle of water. When he came back, the light in the pool had switched itself off. He lay down with her, put one hand to the nape of her neck and closed his eyes. He thought of the colour of the ears of oats that he had rubbed apart with two fingers, and the colour of the reeds beside the boathouse. They were sharp and cut your legs.

'You're still a stranger,' she said.

'I'm sorry,' said Eschburg. Far out to sea he saw the ships, the wandering lights, amber, agate, carnelian, and then he waited for the silence between the sentences they uttered, which was his only measurement of proximity to another human being.

That night, the wind brought sand from Africa, and in the morning everything was covered by a thin, pale yellow layer of it.

21

After a week they flew back separately. Sofia had to go to Paris, Eschburg wanted to return to Berlin. He took a taxi to Linienstrasse from the airport.

He carried his case up to the first floor. His neighbour's door was wide open. Eschburg glanced into her apartment. It was almost empty, with only a sofa and a small table in the middle of the room.

A woman was lying on the sofa. She was naked. Eschburg couldn't see her face; she had laid her head over the arm of the sofa and wasn't moving. For a moment he thought the woman was dead. He was about to go to her, but just then Senja Finks appeared in front of him. She had been standing by the door. She nodded to Eschburg, slowly and seriously. Then she placed her right hand on his chest, pushed him gently back into the hall and closed the heavy door. She did not say a word.

Eschburg went into his apartment, unpacked his case and lay down in bed. He slept restlessly. When he woke at about five in the morning, he felt that he was not alone. The apartment was dark. He waited with his eyes closed, not moving. Suddenly he smelled cedars, and then he felt her breath on his face.

22

Over the next few days Eschburg cleared his studio. He painted the partitions, dealt with his post, took his cameras apart and cleaned them, phoned his publisher and the gallery owner who showed his work, got his hair cut and bought new trousers. He went for long walks in the city and its parks, visited exhibitions and sat in the café for hours without doing anything. He realized that he was taking Sofia's absence badly.

After ten days he flew to Paris. Sofia's agency was holding a reception for an animal protection organization that evening, and Eschburg went straight there from the airport. The reception was in the Hôtel de Crillon on the Place de la Concorde. The women wore long dresses, the men dinner jackets. Eschburg was bored. In the toilets, a young man was taking a line of coke; his left earlobe was stretched out of shape by a bright green silicon earring about twenty millimetres thick. Eschburg went out of the hotel and watched the traffic.

Sofia was able to leave at about one a.m. A driver from the agency took them to her apartment, three tiny rooms in the 10th arrondissement. The first photo that Eschburg had ever taken of her hung over her bed. He had enlarged it to 1.50 by 1.50 metres. It was the only picture in her apartment. Sofia said she was so glad he had come. Then she dropped on the bed and fell asleep at once.

There were sliding glass doors between the bedroom and the living room. He observed Sofia through the glass, and at the same time saw his own reflection: her face on his face. He stood like that for a long time, watching her as she slept.

After the weekend he flew back to Berlin. He went to the State Library and looked for books about Sir Francis Galton, a cousin of Darwin's, who was born in England in the early nineteenth century. Galton invented the weather map and identification by fingerprints. He was convinced that all criminals had visible characteristics distinguishing them from other people. Galton had wondered for a long time how he could illustrate those characteristics, and finally he set up his camera in a London prison and had prisoners brought in. He photographed all their faces on top of each other on a single photographic plate. Galton did not know what evil would look like – it could have shown in the eyes, the foreheads, the ears or the mouths of his subjects. He was astonished when he saw the photograph for the first time: there were no unusual characteristics, and the composite face of all those criminals was a beautiful one.

Eschburg read a lot at this time, filling a book with his notes, and drawing sketches for an installation. After four weeks he booked thirty-eight women from a theatrical agency. His stipulations were few: all the women should be about the same size, they should be between eighteen and twenty-two years old, they were to be dress size 8, and they must be prepared to have nude photographs of themselves taken.

A frame on a wooden platform forced the models to adopt the same physical attitudes for their heads and bodies. Eschburg photographed them one by one from in front with an 8 x 10 Deardorff camera on Polaroid, exposing the photos for fifteen seconds.

The Polaroid pictures were pale grey and looked like soft pencil drawings. The long exposure time made all inessentials disappear, with only the lines of the women's bodies and heads remaining visible. Later, Eschburg had the Polaroids scanned, enlarged to two square metres, and printed on thin Plexiglas plates.

A young man who usually programmed video games for a software company now came to Eschburg's studio every morning. He set up his computer, sat in front of a high-resolution screen, and programmed the installation to Eschburg's instructions. Eschburg got him to explain the principles of his programming. After two months he bought the young man's computer and worked on his own for another eight months. It was a year before the installation was finished. Things were easier with Sofia at this time; they got used to one another, and Eschburg thought he had found the right rhythm for this kind of relationship.

Finally he showed the installation to his gallerist. Eschburg left him and Sofia alone in the studio and went into the inner courtyard. He sat on the steps outside the entrance and peeled an orange, carefully separating the segments. He held the naked fruit up to the sun, turned it, looked at the individual chambers in the flesh, the white skin, the thin veins, orange, yellow and red. He wondered how far it went back, that never-ending number of decisions leading to this moment on the steps. Eschburg slowly closed his hand, the flesh of the fruit was squeezed through his fingers, juice spurted on his shirt, his hair and his face.

23

The entrance to Linienstrasse through the gate in front of Eschburg's building was almost dark. One of the two street lights had been out of order for weeks. All the same, Eschburg could see Senja Finks. A stranger was clutching her throat and pushing her back against the wall. The man was stocky, the nape of his neck shaved; he had broad shoulders and wore a peaked cap. He was stabbing her in the stomach with a knife; he was fast. Eschburg ran.

The stranger drew back to thrust for the second time. Eschburg grabbed the collar of his leather jacket and tore him away from her. The stranger stumbled and lost his balance. Even as he fell, Eschburg turned and hit him. He put all his weight into the blow and struck the stranger's chin. The man's jaw splintered.

Eschburg heard the whirring behind his left ear too late. He couldn't swerve in time. The steel tip of the cudgel hit his head. He was lucky; the angle of impact was low, and the cudgel did not smash his skull. Eschburg fell to his knees. He saw the paving stones, blue-grey with sand and moss between them.

Briefly, the pattern they made intrigued him, and then his forehead hit the ground.

Long before he opened his eyes, he knew he was in a hospital. It was the smell: the mixture of disinfectant, sickness and boiled bed linen.

The first thing he saw was Sofia, sitting by the window with a book. She had taken off her shoes and put her feet up on the windowsill. With the light behind it, her throat looked too slender.

Eschburg didn't want to speak yet; he just looked at her. Finally Sofia put the book down on her lap and audibly breathed out.

'What happened?' he asked. His mouth felt dry, his lips were split.

Sofia came over and kissed him cautiously on the forehead. 'You fell and lost consciousness. You have a hole in your head.'

He tried to move, but the covers on the bed were stiff and heavy.

'You must sleep,' she said. 'They've given you medication.'

Eschburg felt her hand on his forehead; it was cool. He went back to sleep.

When he next woke up it was dark in the room. He sat up in bed and stayed sitting until he was sure he wouldn't feel sick. He was still wearing the hospital smock, but he was not connected to the drip now. He got up and shuffled to the bathroom. There was blood in his urine. His head was bandaged, the right hand side of his face was severely grazed, and he had a dressing over his right eyebrow. He sat on the plastic stool to brush his teeth. It was a strain.

When he came back into the room, there was a woman sitting at the table by the window. It took Eschburg a moment to recognize Senja Finks. She was wearing a dark trouser suit, a pearl necklace and horn-rimmed glasses. Her hair fell loose over her shoulders. The trouser suit looked expensive.

'I waited until your girlfriend left,' she said.

'You look different,' said Eschburg.

'People never see anything but what they want to see.'

Cautiously, Eschburg sat on the edge of the bed. 'You're not injured?'

'It's all right,' she said.

'Who were those men?'

'It's been dealt with,' said Senja Finks.

'What do you mean?'

She shrugged her shoulders and said nothing. Eschburg lay flat on the bed. 'Can you put the light out?' he said. 'It's dazzling me.'

Senja Finks switched the light off. She asked, 'Have you spoken to the police?'

'No,' said Eschburg.

'Then please don't.'

She opened the window. The air was cool and smelled of rain.

He turned his head to her. 'Can you tell me what happened?'

She picked Eschburg's watch up from the bedside table. 'Nice watch. From the sixties?' she asked.

'It was my father's,' he said.

She put the watch down on the table again.

'Please tell me what happened,' said Eschburg.

'It's a long story. You don't want to know.'

'Of course I want to know,' he said.

She looked at him for a long time. 'Very well,' she continued. 'Those men were not pleasant characters, understand? They pick up girls in the villages of Ukraine and promise them a good life. Then they train the girls as prostitutes – "breaking them in", it's called. The girls are made available to punters, often ten or twenty men at a time, mass rapes in empty factory buildings. The police always arrive too late, and by the time they do turn up the girls and their pimps are in the next town. That scene is a world to itself; the punters pay good money, and the pimps are everywhere, in France, Italy, the United Kingdom, Germany. They're quick, those men, and frontiers mean nothing to them at all.'

Senja Finks paused and grimaced. Her shirt was turning dark over her stomach area; her injury had opened up. Her breathing was shallow.

'When a girl is worn out,' said Senja Finks, 'they cut off her hands and her head and throw her away with the garbage. Or they sell her first to a punter who whips her to death. The men record it on video and sell that later.'

'That sort of thing is only for the movies,' said Eschburg.

'No,' she said, 'you won't find it in any movie.'

They both fell silent. Eschburg closed his eyes. His head was hurting.

'Let me ask you now,' said Senja Finks, 'what is a girl like that to do if she's managed to get away? If she's stolen a great deal of money from the men, if she's learned to survive and to kill?'

She stood up and took the two steps over to Eschburg's bed. She smelled of cigarettes and blood. When she leaned forward he saw that her eyes were pale green. Behind the glasses, her pupils were vertical slits.

'What is guilt?' she asked. Her voice sounded feverish.

At close quarters, thought Eschburg, death no longer seems threatening.

'I don't know,' he said.

24

Because Eschburg's photographs aroused more press interest in Italy than anywhere else, the gallery wanted to show his new installation in Rome first. The Japanese who had bought *The Maja's Men* made those two pictures available for the exhibition. The Polaroid plates, the screens, cables and computer were packed into wooden crates in Eschburg's Linienstrasse studio and collected by a haulage firm.

A week later Eschburg flew to Rome. He boarded an airport bus on the runway. Hundreds of starlings were circling the air traffic control tower. Later, his taxi driver told him that Rome was using hawks to try driving those birds out of the city, but the tactic wasn't working.

The gallery had hired the first-floor rooms of a restored seventeenth-century palazzo. Over the next few days, Eschburg made preparations for the exhibition. He hung eighteen photographs along each of the longer walls of the main hall. The Plexiglas plates were lit from behind, showing the women's bodies in a soft, sepia tone. There was a video screen at the end of the hall. The installation was programmed so that a beamer projected one of the Polaroids on to the screen first. A quarter of a second later, the computer laid a second Polaroid over it, making a new picture out of the two of them. Then the next photo was placed on top of that picture, and so on at intervals of a quarter of a second, until the sum of them all was yet another picture. The outcome was that the women photographed by Eschburg merged to form a new woman. Her face and figure were the average of all the models, their central point. All irregularities, folds and blemishes of the skin disappeared. The artificial woman looked younger than the photographic models, her face and body were perfectly symmetrical. And she was indeed beautiful.

Then the Plexiglas plates on the walls had their background lighting switched on, one by one, while the skin of the artificial woman on the screen grew proportionately paler. In the end the only source of light was the plasma screen. Now the artificial woman was almost white. In swift succession she was transformed into the great beauties of art history: Titian's *Venus of Urbino*, Velásquez's *Rokeby Venus*, Canova's *Paolina Borghese*, Manet's *Olympia*, Picasso's *Dryad* and Stuck's *The Sin*. After that she returned to her original form, placed her hands on her back, knelt on the floor, opened her mouth and screamed. Her figure blurred and dissolved, leaving only a white line in the middle of the otherwise black screen. Above the line, translated into all the major languages of the world, appeared Nietzsche's words:

Smooth lies the soul and the sea

The line shrank to a dot, grew pale, and the screen switched itself off. The gallery was left in complete darkness for ten seconds. Then the large Polaroids began glowing gently on the walls again, and the programme started running once more.

Eschburg was invited to appear on a talk show the afternoon before the opening; the gallery owner said they could use the publicity. Before the interview, Eschburg smoked a cigarette on a balcony outside the TV studio. The back yard of the building was full of cardboard cartons torn open, empty flower tubs, and a chair with a broken back.

It was hot in the studio. The presenter spoke fast. An animator signed to the audience, letting them know when to clap. Suddenly the presenter jumped up, flung his arms in the air, and called something out to the spectators, who laughed. The gallery owner had said that the presenter had won a television prize for his 'infectiously human' talk show.

Eschburg saw Sofia. She was sitting in the front row of the audience; he could hardly make out her face.

Then the studio fell silent; the spectators were staring at Eschburg, who seemed to have missed something. Now the presenter was sitting beside him again. He wore a striped yellow and white shirt, with the stripes on the breast pocket mismatched by half a centimetre. Eschburg forced himself not to look at it. The illumination from the floodlights was refracted by a mote of dust on the presenter's rimless glasses.

Eschburg thought of the note he had written in the dark last night. He didn't know just what he had said in it, but he believed it had been important.

Everyone was still waiting. Eschburg smiled because he didn't know what else to do. He wished all this would stop.

At last the presenter was speaking again, clapping his hands once more and turning back to the cameras. Now Eschburg saw a painting on a screen. He didn't understand what the picture had to do with his installation. He heard the woman interpreter's voice; it sounded metallic in the tiny receiver in his ear. 'When is an installation finished?' she was asking. 'When is it finished?'

'When it's right,' Eschburg said at last.

The presenter shouted something at the cameras again; the interpreter didn't translate it. The audience applauded.

At last it was over and the big floodlights were switched off. A sound technician took the microphone off Eschburg's jacket; the hairs on the back of his hand brushed past Eschburg's chin. The presenter was signing autographs for the spectators. He turned round, shook Eschburg's hand and clapped him on the shoulder. Sofia came up on the stage.

At the hotel, Eschburg got under the shower at once. The water tasted of chlorine. He stepped out on to the small balcony with only a towel round his waist. Down in the square a fat man was laughing; he wore a brightly coloured sweatshirt with the words *International Golf Team* embroidered right across its back. He was eating something out of a bag. His wife had no neck.

Eschburg went back into the room and dressed. He found the note he had written last night in a pocket of his jacket. He unfolded it, but the paper was blank.

The exhibition opened the next evening. The models stood under their photographs. Eschburg answered questions from journalists, he talked to guests, art collectors, the ambassador and a State Secretary for Culture.

When he was alone again, he went out on the terrace to smoke. Someone on one side of him offered him a light; he saw only the hand holding it. Eschburg turned.

The young woman's upper lip was the shape of a perfect 'M'. She was wearing a linen dress, and said she had come to Rome on purpose to see his installation. Her voice sounded friendly. Her eyes seemed to consist of different colours, with overlapping layers of green, grey and blue. Later, Eschburg found it impossible to remember their real colour. She was smiling at him.

She held out her hand without giving her name. For a moment her pupils widened, reflecting the light from the hall, and Eschburg saw himself in them. He pulled himself together.

'Sebastian Eschburg,' he said. His face was white.

She went on smiling, but did not let go of his hand. 'I admire your work,' she said. Her face came closer, her voice was lowered. 'I'd very much like to work for you.'

'I never have assistants,' he said. Talking tired him. 'But all right, phone me in Berlin.'

The young woman nodded. At last she let his hand go. 'Many thanks,' she said. 'I won't keep you any longer.'

He waited until he could breathe calmly again. He walked round the exhibition, saw Sofia in the middle of a group of journalists and nodded to her.

The air was better outside. He wandered along the streets. Outside one Renaissance palazzo he stopped and leaned against its stone walls. Then he went on, down to the Tiber and then up into the Trastevere quarter again. He sat down in a street café in the Piazza Santa Maria, and ordered a bottle of water and an espresso. Suddenly he was hearing all the voices in the café simultaneously and at the same volume. He felt as if a filter in his head had stopped working. This lasted about five minutes. The bell of the church of Santa Maria rang at eleven p.m. Its clear, bright sound lingered in the air over the piazza.

Eschburg put some money on the table and stood up. He went back, intending to cross the river over the Ponte Sisto; the yellow lights along the wall of the quay were reflected in the water. He stopped in the middle of the bridge. He saw and heard nothing; he was thinking only of the woman on the terrace. His legs were giving way, he clutched the balustrade of the bridge. A young couple laughed at him, thinking he was drunk. Then he saw Sofia. She was running to him; her face looked to him blurred.

'What's the matter?' she asked. She was breathless. 'I've been looking for you everywhere. You're so pale.'

'I . . . I've been wrong all this time,' he said quietly.

'I don't know what you're talking about,' said Sofia. 'Is it because of the young woman you were with on the balcony?'

'Her skin, I touched her skin. I thought my head was open, my brain all orange and salty.' He was trembling.

'Sebastian,' she said, 'please calm down. Come along, let's go.'

He stayed where he was. 'Those faces and bodies . . . it's only the golden mean . . . ' he said.

'What?'

'The most beautiful face is the most average face. That's all. Beauty is only symmetry. It's so ridiculous. I'm ridiculous.'

'No, you're not ridiculous, you're—'

Eschburg interrupted her. 'When I was very young I went out hunting with my father. He shot a deer. It had been standing in the clearing, calm and beautiful and perfect in itself. He cut through the dead animal's belly, through the coat and the skin and the thin layer of fat. I heard the sound of it. The sound of the body opening up. And I saw the blood, Sofia, all that blood.'

She made as if to put the hair back from his face, but he struck her hand aside.

'That night my father killed himself in his study,' he said.

His face was distorted. He seized her by the shoulders and shook her. 'Don't you understand? I was wrong. It was all wrong. Beauty is not truth.'

'You're hurting me. Stop it,' said Sofia, freeing herself.

'The truth is ugly, it smells of blood and shit. It's the body sliced open, it's my father's head shot away,' said Eschburg.

'You're frightening me, Sebastian,' said Sofia.

He had bought the pocket-knife in France, years ago, and had carried it with him ever since. The paint on the wooden handle had faded, and the maker's name was barely legible. He opened it up.

'What are you doing?' she cried, stepping back.

'Go away,' he said quietly. 'Please, you must go away at once.'

He slid down the balustrade to the ground. The knife cut deeply into the back of his hand.

'I'm frightened myself,' he said.

Red

At one in the morning, Monika Landau was still at the desk in her office. She was forty-one years old, and had been working for the last six years in the capital offences department as one of the public prosecution team. The photograph of the young woman who had been abducted was lying in front of her. TV and the Internet had been showing it for hours. The police had found the photo in the suspect's apartment; he had papered his walls with huge prints of it. He had also painted a red cross on the picture above his bed with his fingers. The report from Forensics said that it was *only* animal blood – a way of putting it that did not reassure anyone.

It had all begun with the call to the police which, like all emergency calls, had been recorded. The caller was a woman; her voice sounded young, at a guess she was about sixteen or seventeen years old. She was frightened, she said, she was lying in the boot of a car. The man had bitten her in the head. She gave the suspect's name and the street where he lived. And then she said something else, in a very low voice, indistinctly. The police thought she had to whisper so that her abductor couldn't hear her. 'He's evil,' said the young woman, or perhaps it was, 'He is the Evil . . . ' Landau couldn't make it out properly. After that the connection was cut.

After the call, a patrol car went to the address; that was routine. The officers found a torn, blood-stained dress in a dustbin in the yard there. That was enough for the investigating magistrate to issue a search warrant. Less than an hour later, investigators were ringing the suspect's doorbell. He opened the door to them. He seemed calm.

They found traces of blood on the floor beside his bed. The forensic pathologist said they matched the blood of the woman whose dress had been found in the dustbin. There was a chest under the bed containing sadistic porn films, handcuffs, whips, blindfolds, gags, vibrators and anal chains. There were scales of skin on the handcuffs and the whips; they, too, came from the unknown woman.

All the equipment one would need for an autopsy was in a metal container in the wardrobe, among the man's shirts: scalpels, clamps, skull splitters, an electric bone saw.

A few hours later, the officers knew that on the day when the woman phoned the police the suspect had hired a car. The police commandeered it from the car hire firm. They found tiny traces of blood in the boot, and again the DNA was the same. The suspect had driven 194 kilometres in the car, so helicopters searched within a radius of a hundred kilometres round Berlin. The choppers, with heat-seeking cameras on board, had been flying over the woods and fields surrounding the city for hours, but they all knew how helpless they were – the area was simply too large. Eight groups of a hundred officers each were engaged in the operation; all police leave in Berlin had been cancelled.

Everything about this case is strange, thought Landau. The investigators didn't know the young woman's name, they didn't know how old she was, where she came from, even who she was. So far there had been no blackmail threats, no demands and no body. Even the suspect didn't fit the usual pattern: he was prosperous and had committed no previous offence. Money could obviously be ruled out as the motive. A pity, thought Landau; it would have made the case easier to understand. Only the clues were straightforward. Landau put on her coat and drove to the police station where the suspect was being held. She would have to question him herself.

The room was on the third floor, bleakly furnished: four chairs, a desk, no pictures, neon lighting. The suspect sat by the window with his right wrist handcuffed to a radiator pipe. This was his third interrogation; so far he had denied everything, but he had not yet asked for a lawyer. The secretarial staff had gone home, so the police officer on duty would have to type up the interview himself. He sat down and switched the computer on.

'So far you've only been provisionally held,' said the police officer to the man. 'In a couple of hours' time the judge will see you and issue a warrant for your detention in custody. This is your last chance to save yourself. Do you remember the caution we gave you? You don't have to answer any questions here and now.'

The public prosecutor was seeing the suspect for the first time. She nodded to him. He did not react.

'Where's the girl?' asked the police officer.

'I don't know,' said the man.

'Listen, we don't have to begin at the beginning all over again. We know you abducted the woman. So stop beating about the bush. What have you done with her? Where is she? What's her name?'

'I don't know,' repeated the man.

'Is she still alive? Have you locked her up somewhere? Does she have enough warm clothing? Water? Food? Have you any idea how cold it is tonight? Minus nine degrees. She'll freeze if you've left her out of doors.'

The police officer had not typed anything on the computer yet. There was no recorder in the room, and no video camera.

Interrogations, reflected Landau, are complicated. Why would anyone confess at all? If the perpetrator of a crime stops to think for a moment, he knows that he'll lose by confessing. A man confesses to a crime only if he's going to get something in return − maybe a more lenient sentence, or the relief of having unburdened his conscience, the prospect of sleeping peacefully without nightmares. Or sometimes he just wants the recognition of the officer questioning him. Landau believed that only good experiences in childhood can ultimately lead to a confession. She had conducted many interrogations; she knew how difficult it is to tell the truth.

The police officer told the man he would never be able to look at his own face in the mirror again; night after night he would see the young woman there, she would follow him all his life. What he had done was bad, but he could still redeem himself.

Any judge would be more lenient if he talked now, if he told the whole story and saved the girl. The police officer was talking to him quietly, in a monotone, repeating what he said again and again.

The interrogation had gone on for over three hours when it happened. 'I have two daughters myself,' said the police officer. 'They're twelve and fourteen years old.' His voice had changed; he was speaking very quietly.

Landau sat up and took notice. She didn't understand what the police officer was doing. Of course a clever officer forfeits his power during an interrogation. He has to get the criminal to trust him. If the interrogating officer is enraged or horrified, or forgets for a moment that he is speaking to another human being, he won't get anywhere. A police interrogator can go very far and risk a good deal in such circumstances. Landau had heard interrogations when she almost thought a kind of friendship was developing between the police officer and the criminal. But no interrogator brings his private life into it, she thought now. That's too dangerous.

The police officer got to his feet, picked up his chair by its back and carried it round the table. It was a metal chair, and he slammed it down on the floor right in front of the suspect. Then he turned briefly to Landau and shrugged his shoulders. It looked like an apology, but Landau didn't know how to take it.

The police officer sat down. The suspect raised his eyebrows and looked at the other man. The officer leaned forward. His face was less than thirty centimetres from the suspect's.

'You wanted it this way,' said the police officer. 'I'll explain to you first. I want you to know exactly what I'm going to do to you.'

Landau realized that the situation was getting out of control. Later, she often thought of this moment, and then she wondered whether she could have prevented it. But she always came to the same conclusion: she hadn't wanted to.

'These days,' said the police officer, 'we don't do it with electric shocks to your balls, or knives, or beatings. That's Hollywood stuff. All I need is a kitchen towel and a bucket of water. It's fast. We're on our own here, you bastard, the others are out searching for the girl. If you say what happened later, no one will believe you. You won't have any visible injury, no scars, there'll be no blood, it will all be inside your head. Of course you'll call a doctor later, but he won't be able to establish anything. It'll be my word against yours. You don't even need to wonder which of us the judge will believe. You're a rapist and now you're going to pay for it. No one holds out against what I'm going to do to you for more than thirty seconds. Most of them give up after three or four. You will ...'

At that moment Landau managed to stand up, and she left the room without a word. She walked down the brightly lit corridor to the toilets. She closed the door of the ladies behind her and leaned against it. The place smelled of chlorine and liquid soap. When she had calmed down, she put her handbag on the shelf and washed her face, bending over the basin to let cold water run over the nape of her neck. She folded a paper towel, moistened it and pressed it to her eyes. Then she went to the window and opened it.

'I swear that in the exercise of my office I will be faithful to the Basic Law of the Federal Republic of Germany and the constitution of the city of Berlin, in accordance with the law and for the good of the general public, and I swear to carry out my official duties conscientiously, so help me God.' She had taken that oath twelve years ago, and she still knew it by heart. 'So help me God.' Most of the younger public prosecutors left that clause out; everyone had a free choice there. But she had said it; she still retained her childhood belief in a kind, omnipotent deity.

She looked out at the inner courtyard of the old building. It was dark, and there were lights on in only a few of the rooms. She took a deep breath. The air was so cold that it hurt her lungs. She closed the window again, sat on the radiator, took one of her shoes off and massaged her foot. She hadn't slept for twenty-six hours.

She thought of the trial in which she had been involved four years before. A jealous husband had tipped boiling milk over his wife's breasts, intending to punish her. Landau had prosecuted the husband, but during the trial the wife had killed herself. After that case, Landau had wanted to give up. But her head of department had said something that she felt was both horrifying and consoling, and she had borne it in mind every day since then. 'We don't win cases, we don't lose cases, we do our job,' he had said.

All at once Landau sat up straight. Suddenly she was wide awake, with her mind perfectly clear. She hurried out of the ladies, down the corridor, and pushed the door of the interrogation room open. She had left the police officer and the suspect together for twenty-four minutes.

*

Later, Landau was sitting alone with the police officer in the neon-lit canteen. He was one of the most experienced officers in the Berlin police force, fifteen years older than Landau. She had known him ever since she began working in the capital crimes department. She knew that he was thoughtful and reserved, he had never drawn his gun, his judgement was flawless. She asked him why he had done it. He had not said anything yet. He pulled the paper label off a bottle of water, stuck it to the table and smoothed it out. He stared at the label, but he still said nothing.

At last he began to speak. He told her about another case of abduction, eighteen years ago.

'I still remember every detail,' said the police officer, without looking at Landau. 'I remember the gold bracelet on the man's wrist, the loose button on his shirt, his thin lips and the way he drummed his fingers on the table. After two days we got to the point where he said he would show us the place in the forest. I was sitting beside him as we drove there. He smelled unwashed, he had saliva in the corners of his mouth and he was coughing. And grinning, but all the same I had to be friendly to him. "Twelve days before Christmas." Those words kept going round in my head all through the drive to the forest. It was about as cold as today. When we got there, a colleague of mine spotted the ventilation pipe and ran to it. He was tearing off his jacket as he ran. He scraped the leaves off the pipe, he was shouting that everything would be all right now. We all dropped to our knees beside that pipe and dug like crazy in the snow and the frozen ground. Another of my colleagues broke the crate open. I saw the scratches the little boy had left inside its lid. There was a red transfer on his forearm, some kind of animal, an elephant or a rhinoceros, maybe something else. The picture was ragged at the edges and washed-out; it looked so unreal on the child's bluish-white skin.'

The police officer raised his head and looked directly at Landau. 'You see, it's that damn transfer. I can't get it out of my mind. Do you understand that? I just can't get it out of my mind.'

On the afternoon of that day, Public Prosecutor Landau wrote a memo in her office. It was not long, twelve lines. She read it again twice, signed it and pinned the sheet of paper to the files. Then she went to the registry and asked one of the secretarial staff there to fax her memo to the interrogating officers.

'In what case?' asked the secretary.

'The new one. The file on it is in my office,' said Landau. 'The accused is called Sebastian von Eschburg.'

Blue

1

Konrad Biegler was standing moodily on the terrace of the Zirmerhof hotel, listening to the mountain guide. The man looked exactly as Biegler would have imagined a mountain guide: tanned brown, tall, healthy. He'll certainly smell of soap, thought Biegler. The mountain guide had a firm voice with a slight Italian accent; it sounded pleasant. The terrace of the hotel, he said, was 'almost 1,600 metres above sea level', the panoramic view was 'unique, about a hundred peaks' that 'made the heart lift'. Up here, he added, there were 'wonderful meadows' and 'idyllic mountain lakes'.

The mountain guide made many more such remarks. He wore a red polyester jacket with a hood and a fox on the breast pocket. Functional clothing, thought Biegler. The mountain guide named the ranges here: 'Brenta, Ortler, Ötztaler, Stubaier.' Biegler was sure the guide had climbed them all.

A woman with a very small rucksack said quietly that the Zirmerhof was as high up as the Schneekoppe, the highest peak in the Czech Republic. Her eyes shone as she looked at the mountain guide. 'Except that this hotel doesn't have snow on it,' said Biegler, buttoning up his coat.

Biegler had been a defence lawyer in Berlin for thirty-one years. He was allergic to grass, hay, dogs, cats and horses. He wondered whether to make a comment. For instance, 'We Germans always rate nature above other human beings.' But he didn't. It was nothing to do with him. He wasn't going to have to live in the mountains; some time he could leave this place and go back to Berlin. The city is the right place for human beings, he thought. Biegler pulled himself together. 'Relax,' the doctor had told him.

In the middle of a trial four weeks ago, Biegler had fallen over one evening, just like that, in the corridor of the Central Criminal Court in Berlin, the Moabit. He had hit his forehead on a stone parapet and slipped to the floor. The doctor had sent him to a hospital where he and other patients suffering from 'burn-out' sat in a circle, throwing brightly coloured woolly balls to each other; in the afternoons he was supposed to cut shapes out of paper. Biegler had discharged himself after two days.

'Then at least go to the mountains,' the doctor had insisted. Preferably the South Tyrol. The doctor had read something out of a brochure: at this hotel, the Zirmerhof, it said, peace was understood as something more than 'the absence of noise', it was an 'inner quality maintaining life'. Many famous people, the doctor assured him, had come to this mountain hotel to recuperate. He reeled off the names of Heisenberg, Planck, Feltrinelli, Trott zu Solz, Siemens, and a whole series of artists and writers. Eugen Roth had even written a poem about the hotel. Biegler booked a room.

Now the hotel guests were leaving the terrace with the mountain guide. Biegler stood up, arching his back. All the chairs at the Zirmerhof were uncomfortable, and he wondered whether there was some ulterior reason for it. The other guests − most of them mountain walkers − thought it weak-minded to sit on the cushions meant for the outdoor chairs. Biegler always took two of them.

He got a book out of his coat pocket. The doctor had not forbidden him to read. Biegler opened the book. He had been here for four days, but he still couldn't concentrate on it. It was called *Positive Thinking For Managers*. His former secretary had given it to him as a goodbye present, saying that it would do him good. By now Biegler owned a considerable collection of such books. *Feeling, Thinking and Acting in Harmony With the Universe*; *The Power of Good Feelings*; *Living More Consciously, With 30 Motivational Maps and Online Materials*; *Seven Steps to Congeniality*; and finally Biegler's favourite title: *Positive Thinking: Walking To Success. Mental Training For Your Personal Victory*. His secretary had just retired, and he had seen her successor only once.

Biegler's wife Elly also despaired of his dismal mood. They had been married for twenty-eight years. Elly thought Biegler's grouchiness was the result of his career and the murder trials in which he acted for the defence. However, she was wrong; Biegler simply considered 'positive thinking' a stupid idea. He had tried to wean the junior lawyers in his chambers off it. Good-tempered people, he thought, were either childish or sneaky.

A farmer was mowing the meadow in front of the terrace. His tractor was a fine-looking machine, but there was something wrong with its exhaust. Biegler thought there was something wrong with the farmer too – he mowed the same part of the meadow every day. He tried the positive-thinking trick and said a civil good morning to the farmer. The farmer stared blankly at him. Biegler nodded, satisfied.

He walked a little way. Over fifty larchwood benches stood round the hotel. As a guest at the Zirmerhof, you could buy the right to have your name burned on one of these benches by the village joiner. Biegler tried them, one by one. They were always placed so that he was obliged to look at the allegedly idyllic sights: mountains, meadows, trees, footpaths, rocks. Biegler's mood darkened from bench to bench.

He didn't want to disappoint Elly. He went to his room, which was no larger than the conference table in his chambers. Briefly, he entertained the notion of calling the hotelier and pointing out that the juridical system condemned the imprisonment of miscreants in cells smaller than twelve square metres as an offence against human dignity. He didn't, because he was supposed to be recuperating. Elly had bought him hiking boots with red soles. Biegler shook his head and put them on.

A narrow path behind the hotel led into the forest. The undergrowth smelled musty; tiny living creatures were always ready to jump out at him from the tree trunks. He was sweating. There were cows in a large clearing; they belonged to the hotel. The hotelier had said they were docile. Biegler didn't trust the hotelier, and kept his distance. Surely the cows must be deafened by the huge cowbells around their necks. He watched them until he felt sure that cows were not a sentient life form.

Biegler turned and went back to the hotel. He showered and lay down on the bed. Twenty minutes later, building work for a new flight of steps outside the hotel began under his window. The construction workers were listening to the radio. He opened the window and lit a cigarillo. A chambermaid knocked on his door and warned him that smoking in the rooms was forbidden. You could smell it out in the corridor, she said.

Two hours later, a cowbell rang to announce that it was time for supper.

A man in short lederhosen was sitting at the table next to his. The man moved jerkily, and had a yellowish dog that he called Wolf. The man's wife had short hair and a massive face with jowls. When Biegler saw that the man had a huge knife with a horn handle in his belt, he asked to be seated somewhere else.

He was shown to the table of a married couple of teachers from Stuttgart. They were talking about today's hike, and addressed each other by pet names. Supper was baked cheese dumplings in tomato sauce. The waitress sprinkled parmesan on them. Biegler wasn't sure whether he would be able to eat the dumplings.

The husband asked Biegler whether he, too, had been out hiking that day.

'Yes,' said Biegler.

'You really must go up the Weisshorn. There's a wonderful view,' said the wife, whom her husband addressed as Treasure.

'Yes,' said Biegler again. Fat from the cheese dumplings splashed on to his shirt.

'Or go to the Bletterbach Ravine. UNESCO has named it a

World Heritage Geopark. You can see mineral strata millions of years old there – it's fantastic.'

Biegler did not reply, but Treasure wasn't giving up. 'You haven't been here long, have you?'

'Four days,' said Biegler. He asked the waitress for bread, dry bread.

'You can get a hiking map at reception,' said the husband. 'It's helpful the first time you go out.'

'Thanks,' said Biegler.

'What have you seen so far?' asked Treasure.

'The village graveyard. I like those enamel pictures of the dead. They look so lifelike,' said Biegler.

'Oh?' Treasure sounded uncertain of herself. 'Would you like to join us? We're going up to the pass tomorrow.' She smiled at him. She wore no makeup, and had a healthy pink skin.

'No,' said Biegler.

'Don't you like hill-walking, then?' asked the male teacher. His glasses were steamed up with condensation from the food.

'No.'

The couple stared at him. In such situations Elly usually saved the day, but Elly wasn't here. Biegler put down his knife and fork. 'Why do you like nature?' he asked.

'What kind of question is that?' asked the teacher, laughing. 'Everyone loves nature.'

'I don't,' said Biegler. 'And you haven't answered the question.'

'Why do I love nature?' the teacher repeated.

'We need nature, but nature doesn't need us,' said Treasure. She spoke sternly.

'That sounds like a bumper-sticker slogan,' said Biegler.

'Wait a minute ... I know you from somewhere,' said the

teacher, who had pulled himself together again. 'Yes, now I know – I saw you on television. You were defending that murderer in Cologne who killed his whole family.'

'No, that wasn't me,' said Biegler untruthfully. He didn't like the turn this conversation was taking. 'I still don't understand why you like nature.'

'It's so beautiful and restful to go hiking,' said Treasure. 'And . . . '

'And nature is much cleverer than we are,' said her husband.

'Nonsense,' said Biegler. 'Think of eels.'

'Eels?' asked Treasure, making a face. She didn't seem to be keen on eels.

'Eels are perfect for understanding nature,' said Biegler. 'It's like this: every eel you see in Europe was born in the Atlantic, in the Sargasso Sea near the Bahamas. The larvae swim from there to Europe. It takes them about three years. Understand? For three years all they do is swim across the sea. On the coast they grow larger, swim up the rivers, wriggle over some damp water meadows, and finally spend the next twenty years living in a stretch of water somewhere. All that's crazy enough, but now it gets disgusting. The eel stops eating, and changes. Its eyes get larger, its stomach and anus disappear, and huge sexual organs form in it. Believe me, they really are huge. They fill the entire eel, you could even say the whole eel is now a single sexual organ. And what does it do?'

The teachers stared at Biegler.

'It has to go back,' said Biegler. 'Five thousand kilometres back by way of water meadows, rivers and seas, until it reaches the Sargasso Sea. At last, half dead with exhaustion, it arrives. The other eels are already there. It dives half a kilometre down into the water, has sex for the one and only time in its life – in the dark, of course – and dies.' Biegler pushed his plate aside and waited for a moment. 'I only mean to say that I don't think nature thought up any sensible ideas for the eels. In fact I'm pretty sure nature never thought up anything at all. Nature doesn't think, it's hostile or at best indifferent. So to answer your question: many thanks for the invitation, but I have no desire at all to climb any mountains or look at mineral strata millions of years old.'

Biegler stood, nodded to the couple, and went up to his room.

It was still light outside. The meadow fell steeply away outside his window, down to a pool of water in a hollow in the ground. A duck was slowly swimming round in circles there; the water was black. He heard a gnat behind his ear, closed the window and got his thumb wedged in it.

It soon felt stuffy in the tiny room; a smell of cleaning fluid came from the plastic shower. He looked for the gnat, couldn't find it, showered, put his pyjamas on and got into bed. Reading the hotel brochure, he saw that it offered an 'Alpine hay-bath' for 'that fresh, comfortable sensation'. Biegler thought of his allergy to hay. He wondered whether Elly would believe him if he claimed to have an allergy to mountain air.

Biegler closed his eyes. He saw himself frolicking over the newly mown meadow with the man in lederhosen, the massive woman and the two teachers, naked in the morning dew. Then he fell asleep.

2

Biegler was woken by the sound of a delivery van's engine. He had opened the window again in the night and now the room smelled of diesel. He looked at his watch: just before six. He tried dropping off to sleep again. A few minutes later the church bells began ringing for early Mass. Biegler groaned and sat up. He took his coat off the hook, put it on over his pyjamas, and went outside in his slippers.

It was cool. He lit a cigarillo. Around now Elly would be having breakfast in her conservatory. She went to her practice at eight. He called her.

'I'm bored,' he said.

'Don't you like it there at all?'

'It's a Magic Mountain for senior teachers.'

'Have you been out walking?'

'Every day. I'm fine now, fit as a fiddle. I could come home.'

'You ought to stay there a while longer, Biegler,' said Elly. She said it gently. She always called him Biegler.

'You know, the food here is horrible. It gives me indigestion the whole time,' said Biegler.

'At least another three weeks,' she said.

He knew that tone of voice; for all her gentle manner, she could be stern. He drew on his cigarillo and coughed.

'And you ought to smoke less.'

They said goodbye. Biegler put his phone in his coat pocket. He wished he were in his regular café on Savignyplatz now. He imagined reading the newspaper there, eating a croissant and watching people in the street.

Recently Elly had spoken quite often of a round-the-world trip. He liked the idea of seeing other countries, but as soon as he was really there he hated them. There was something different wrong every time: the beds, his digestion, the heat, the insects, the mode of transport. He also refused to bathe in the sea; in his opinion, dry land was the natural habitat of human beings.

Biegler smoked for a little longer. He was feeling afraid that he would never be allowed back into a courtroom again. He put his cigarillo down in an ashtray where rainwater had gathered overnight.

After breakfast – Biegler was just drinking his second cup of coffee on the terrace – his phone rang. Not recognizing the ring tone, he ignored it. Only when the other guests looked at him, and a man raised his eyebrows, did he place the sound. His secretary was calling. Biegler's office manager had taken her on, saying that she was very capable. Biegler had seen her only briefly on her first working day, because after that he had been in hospital. She was young, pretty and intelligent.

'Good morning, Herr Biegler,' she said. 'How is your holiday going?'

She has a nice voice, too, thought Biegler. Someone will fall in love with her and marry her, she'll get pregnant, and I'll have to pay for it all.

'Are you recuperating?' she asked.

'No one ever recuperates on holiday,' said Biegler. 'Why are you calling?'

'Wait a moment, I'll put your colleague on the line.'

One of the young lawyers from his chambers came to the phone. 'We're sorry to disturb you, Herr Biegler, but we can't make the decision without you.'

'What decision?' asked Biegler.

'We had a call from the remand prison this morning. An inmate wants you to take on his defence. His girlfriend has been here already; finance won't be any problem.'

'What's the charge?'

'Murder. It's that big case; the press had a field day, printing new stories on the subject almost every day. It was about five months ago. He killed a woman.'

'Is said to have killed a woman,' said Biegler.

'What?'

'He's *said* to have killed a woman. That's what we say until he's found guilty: *said* to have done so-and-so. Good heavens, what do they teach you lot these days?'

'Sorry.'

'Has he been charged yet?'

'Yes, a month ago. The court is about to set the dates for the trial.'

'Which courtroom?'

'The 14th Criminal Court.'

'Who's appearing for the prosecution?'

137

'Monika Landau.'

'Do I know her?'

'She's been with Capital Crimes for six years. Came from Narcotics, before that she was with Robbery. She's considered to be fair. But we haven't faced her in a trial ourselves before.'

'Tall, dark-haired woman? Early forties?'

'Yes, that's her.'

'I remember,' said Biegler. 'Who's doing the psychiatric report?'

'No one so far. The client refused to see a psychiatrist.'

'Sounds interesting,' said Biegler, 'but I'm stuck here, can't get away.'

'Yes, that's what we thought too. But then we found that memo in the files, and we decided to call you.'

'What memo?'

'Until now the client's been represented by a lawyer from Legal Aid. We don't know whether the Legal Aid guy failed to notice the memo or whether he just didn't bother about it. Anyway, the press hasn't mentioned it yet.'

'Again, please: what memo?'

At that moment the farmer with the defective tractor drove past the terrace. Biegler pressed his phone to his ear to hear what the young lawyer was saying, and shouted at him to speak up. Then he said, 'Don't fax the memo to me here – not secure enough. I'm leaving at once. I'll be at the Bayerischer Hof in Munich this evening, so you can send it there by courier. Apply for a review of the remand order. And then find someone in the office to summarize the files for me, and let me have the summary the day after tomorrow. I ought to be at chambers around two in the afternoon.'

'Yes, I'll see to all that.'

'I'll be in touch,' said Biegler, and ended the call without saying goodbye.

The hotelier charged Biegler for all the days he had booked. Tap water appeared on the invoice as 'Zirmerhof Water' at a cost of two euros per jug. Biegler was irate, and quoted Montaigne's comments on landlords in his travel journal. Even then, he pointed out to the hotelier, they had a reputation as cut-throats.

He was glad to be sitting in his car. Halfway down to the valley he stopped, got out, and walked through the apple orchards along a gravel path. After a while he took his jacket off and carried it over his arm. He picked an apple from a branch, ate it, and wiped the back of his neck with a handkerchief. Two hours later, tired from walking, he sat down on a rock. There was no wind, and his shoes were dusty. Biegler's mind was at ease. He thought of his sixtieth birthday last year. A friend had given him a steel tube, saying that it would survive even nuclear war. 'Put the things you want to outlast you in it and bury it in your garden.' The tube had spent a week lying on Biegler's desk, and then he had thrown it away.

Driving over the Brenner Pass, he listened to jazz. Bill Evans, *Explorations*; Dave Brubeck, *Time Out*; Herbie Hancock, *The New Standard*. When he was seventeen he'd wanted to be a musician himself. He had appeared at clubs then, playing jazz trumpet. Audiences liked his rounded, mellow tone. But then he had met Albert Mangelsdorff with his gigantic trombone. Mangels-dorff used to play and sing into the mouthpiece at the same time. Biegler had known at once that he himself would never play again.

He put off phoning Elly until he was over the border between Italy and Austria. She was cross, of course. 'Oh, really, you're hopeless, Biegler,' she said.

Three hours later, Biegler was parking in front of the Bayerischer Hof hotel in Munich. 'Civilization at last,' he said, meaning room service. He over-tipped the concierge.

Although he usually showered, now he lay in the bathtub for almost an hour. When the floor waiter delivered the envelope to his room, he was still in his dressing gown. Biegler found his reading glasses, sat at the desk and read the memo. He lay down on the sofa. He knew how sick he really was, but he had to go back. They've gone too far, he thought.

3

On the morning of the next day but one, Biegler got up at six. He had read the files overnight, and had not slept much, but all the same he felt better, refreshed. He had breakfast with Elly.

'The tree expert was here last week,' Elly said from behind her newspaper.

'The what?'

'Tree expert. If you want to fell a tree in Berlin you have to get permission from a tree expert.'

'Oh God,' said Biegler.

'He said the tree is perfectly healthy, so you can't chop it down,' said Elly.

The tree stood outside the conservatory where he and Elly breakfasted every morning. It cast a gloomy light into the room.

'Does that mean I have to go on living in the shade?'

'So to speak, yes,' said Elly.

'We Germans are truly crazy,' said Biegler. 'I'll poison the tree. Lead poisoning. How do I go about it?'

Elly didn't reply.

'I could call one of my clients and get him to shoot the tree,' said Biegler.

'Do stop making such a fuss,' said Elly.

Two years ago, Elly had sent him to a psychoanalyst. He was getting more and more impossible, she had said. He went, and sat listening to the analyst breathing for eight sessions. Each session cost him 85 euros. Naturally Biegler hadn't said a word. Thinking about himself bored him to death. After spending 680 euros he had broken off the analysis. He dared not tell Elly, and had been living ever since in the fear that she would find out. He had bought Freud's *Collected Works*, and sometimes quoted from them. He hoped to get by like that.

'It says in the paper you've taken on the case of that artist,' said Elly.

'I may.'

'They write that he probably did commit the murder.'

'Otherwise it wouldn't be news,' said Biegler.

Elly suggested that he might take the new secretary flowers, but he declined to. 'Flowers are open sexual organs; I don't give that kind of thing to anyone, particularly not a young woman,' he said.

At eight he went to the Moabit remand prison. At reception he showed his authorization as Eschburg's defence counsel and asked to see his client. The woman police officer telephoned, and then asked Biegler if he felt better for his holiday. Biegler didn't reply to that.

At the moment, said the officer, Eschburg was the most famous prisoner on remand there. He was very calm, she said, and spent most of his time lying on the bed in his cell. He was polite to the officers on duty and the other inmates. So far, she added, he hadn't complained of anything or asked for any kind of special treatment.

'Sounds pleasant enough,' said Biegler.

'There's something strange about him,' said the woman officer.

'What?' asked Biegler.

'I don't really know,' she said. 'It's just a kind of feeling.'

'A feeling,' repeated Biegler. The woman officer nodded.

After a few minutes Eschburg arrived. Biegler took him into one of the interview rooms kept for lawyers and their clients.

'Do you smoke?' asked Biegler.

'I've given up in here,' said Eschburg.

Biegler put his cigarillos away again. 'Smoking in these interview rooms is forbidden anyway. You've asked me to take on your defence.'

'Yes.'

'You already have a defence counsel from Legal Aid.'

'But now I need you,' said Eschburg.

'Why?'

'Everyone out there thinks I'm a murderer.'

'Well, you did confess,' said Biegler.

'Yes.'

'And you signed your confession.'

'Yes, but that was under duress.'

'Do you mean that your confession isn't true?'

'I'd like you to defend me as if I were not the murderer.'

'As if you were *not* the murderer? Do I understand you correctly? Are you or are you not a murderer?'

'Is that important?'

It was a good question. Biegler had never heard a client ask it before. Journalists ask such questions, he thought, students or legal interns. 'It's not important for the defence, if that's what you mean,' said Biegler.

'And for you personally?'

'In defending a case, only the defence matters.'

'That's why I want you to defend me. Not all lawyers see it that way.' Eschburg seemed perfectly calm. 'Have you read the files?' he asked.

'I've seen worse,' said Biegler.

'How would you defend me?'

Biegler looked at Eschburg. 'If one is aiming for a verdict of not guilty to a charge of murder, there are six possibilities. One: it was right to kill – that line of defence is very unusual. Two: it was self-defence. Three: it was an accident. Four: you didn't know what you were doing; in effect, you couldn't tell right from wrong when you did it. Five: it wasn't you, some-one else committed the murder. And six – also very unusual – there wasn't a murder at all. To sum up, briefly: for now, we can leave aside self-defence, accident and the inability to tell right from wrong for the time being. So let's begin with the alternative murderer theory. Who, if not you, could have done it?'

Eschburg thought for a little while. 'No one.'

'Don't you have any neighbours?' asked Biegler.

'Yes, a woman called Senja Finks,' said Eschburg.

'Tell me about her.'

Eschburg told him what he knew about her, including the knife attack and her injuries.

144

'Right,' said Biegler. He wrote it all down in his notebook. 'I can think about that. Now we come to the last possible defence, and in this case the most interesting one: there has been no murder.'

'But I confessed.'

'So you did.'

'But?' asked Eschburg.

'The prosecution will do everything possible to get that confession accepted in court. But I suspect that the court of first instance won't want to evaluate it. In that case the judges in your full trial will have to decide whether the other evidence is enough on its own to arraign you. There are some open questions. The two most important are: who was the woman victim? And where is her body? Your confession stops short at that point.'

'Do I have to answer the court's questions?'

'No.' Biegler opened the file. 'Here's the last thing you said: "I made the body disappear. I disposed of it." That's the end of the interrogation.' Biegler turned the file to Eschburg and showed him the place.

'I remember,' said Eschburg.

'How did you do it?'

'What?'

'The disappearing trick? Like Houdini the magician?'

'With chemicals.'

'Aha.'

'As a photographer I have access to them.'

'Go on.'

'I put the body in a bath of hydrochloric acid. It dissolved,' said Eschburg.

Biegler picked up the file again and put it back in his bag. He stood up. 'No, I don't think I will agree to defend you.'

'Why not?'

At last, thought Biegler. For the first time, I've got a reaction out of him. 'Because I don't believe you. Of course you don't have to tell me the truth. You can deny everything. You can say nothing, you can even try out different versions of a story on me. Lies are in order. But one thing I can't stand, and that is clients confessing to something they did *not* do.'

'I don't understand,' said Eschburg.

'Bodies dissolved in hydrochloric acid – that kind of thing belongs in a crime novel. It doesn't work, or at least not particularly well. Even after many days in a bath of hydrochloric acid, a body doesn't dissolve entirely. The liquid turns yellowish, there are clumps of organic matter left. Not to mention teeth and bones.'

'How about that case in Belgium – the pastor?' asked Eschburg.

'You found out the details of that? Interesting. You mean András Pándy, the Hungarian,' said Biegler, while he put his coat on. 'Yes, Pándy killed four of his eight children. But he didn't use hydrochloric acid, he used drain cleaner to dispose of the bodies. You could buy the heavy-duty sort in any pharmacy at the time. Pándy's daughter confessed to doing it. She was not a very likeable character herself. She shot her mother so that she could go on sleeping with her father as before.'

Biegler was pacing up and down the room in his coat, with his hands behind his back, a posture he sometimes adopted when he gave guest lectures at the Police College.

'At least, the young woman claimed to have taken the bodies

apart, put them in drain cleaner, and then washed everything away down the plug-hole. No one believed that story. The Belgian investigating magistrate wanted to check it. As far as I know, that's the only time such a procedure has been scientifically tested.'

'Did it work?'

'In an experiment, pigs' heads were taken apart and put into the drain cleaning solution first. It was astonishing; they did indeed dissolve entirely within twenty-four hours: teeth, hair, bones and all. After that the method was tested on human remains, not a pleasant business, and ethically dubious into the bargain. I published an article on it. The experiment with human body parts went just like the experiment with the pigs' heads. Everything dissolved entirely and very quickly. The drain cleaner was made in England; its brand name was Cleanest.' Biegler smiled. 'Kind of suitable, don't you think?'

He stopped pacing up and down, stood beside Eschburg and leaned forward. 'But that was in 1998, fourteen years ago. When the experiment was made known publicly, the manufacturer of Cleanest changed the composition of the cleaner, and hydrochloric acid had never been part of it.'

Biegler found it unsettling to see how much his own impression of Eschburg differed from the accounts of him given in the files. The young man was not cold. It was something else: Eschburg seemed to be waiting for something, but Biegler didn't know what it was. 'So don't fool yourself,' he said. 'You probably wouldn't even be capable of taking a body apart. It's far from easy. And now I must be going.'

'Please, wait a moment,' said Eschburg. He took a press cutting out of his jacket and put it on the table. Biegler picked it up. It was an article about him. He had been acting for the defence in a case of rape at the time.

'So? There are better-known lawyers,' he said.

'I'm not bothered about that. You said in that interview that truth and reality were entirely different things, in the same way as justice and morality were different. Did you say that only because it sounds good?' Like most remand prisoners, Eschburg was pale. He was wearing a black cashmere jacket and a black roll-neck sweater, which further intensified his pallor.

'It says in this article that you really wanted to be a musician, but then you began studying law.' Eschburg read aloud. '"The law courts are the last major institution to concentrate on the subject of truth," you said. That's why I want you to defend me.'

'All that was a long time ago,' said Biegler. 'You're accused of murder. You ought to be devoting your mind exclusively to yourself.'

'I am,' said Eschburg. 'Will you defend me?'

'Because reality and truth are two different things?' asked Biegler.

'Because you understand that,' said Eschburg.

Biegler looked at the time. He sat down again. 'Very well, then. I think your case is interesting. But not because of the alleged absence of a body, and certainly not because you're a well-known artist. All that interests me in your case is the question of torture.'

'Do you want me to describe it?'

'No,' said Biegler. 'Counsel for the prosecution in this case has written a memo on the subject. It all depends on that and nothing else. I'm afraid the court wouldn't believe you if you told a different story. For now, that memo is enough for me. I have an engagement to see both the lawyer from the public prosecutor's office and the presiding judge in your case tomorrow. The day after tomorrow the review of your remand in custody takes place. So, we'll see. I'll get the people here to bring you copies of the files today.'

Biegler left the remand prison by way of the cellar staircase to the courthouse building. Wet leaves were lying in the street and sticking to the bonnets of cars, and the large window panes of the buses were clouded with condensation.

Maybe that police officer was right, thought Biegler, and there's something wrong with the man. Eschburg couldn't have got hold of that newspaper article after he was remanded in custody; he must have read it earlier. Suddenly Biegler felt that pressure in his chest again. The pain moved on over his shoulder and up to his lower jaw. He waited for the pressure to slacken. Although it was chilly, he took off his coat.

He went through the little park to the church. He hadn't been in a church for years, not since his son's christening. The door was open. He took off his hat and sat down in the last pew at the back. The church was empty, and light fell, slanting, through the yellow windows to the floor. Someone had scratched his initials on the pew. There was a crack in a flag-stone on the floor. He passed his shoe over it. For a while he stayed there, staring at the flagstone.

Outside the church, a boy was repairing his bicycle on the pavement. He had turned it upside down, handlebars and saddle on the ground, and was pushing the pedals to make the back wheel go round. It was unbalanced. The boy's hands were dirty and one elbow was grazed. He was trying to straighten the wheel with his forearms.

'You're not going to get it straight that way,' said Biegler. The boy looked up at him. Biegler shrugged. 'That's life,' he said. The boy went on trying. Biegler watched for a little longer, then pulled his wallet out of his jacket and gave the boy a twenty-euro note. 'Buy yourself a new wheel rim,' he said. The boy took the money and put it in his pocket, without saying anything.

4

'Almond biscuit?' The presiding judge offered a biscuit tin, holding it out over his desk. He wore a blue blazer with gilt buttons that had a fancy coat of arms engraved on them. He was smooth-shaven, with a pink skin, a double chin and ears that stuck out. He wore round-rimmed glasses that were too large for him. Those who didn't know him thought he was a friendly soul, perhaps slightly stupid.

'My wife made them,' said the presiding judge.

Landau shook her head, Biegler helped himself to a biscuit. It tasted like cardboard. Biegler remembered that a few years ago, the presiding judge had had an affair with a woman studying to qualify as a judge. Rumour said that it had cost him his appointment to the Federal High Court.

'Thank you very much,' said Biegler.

The presiding judge watched Biegler munching. 'She's wonderful at baking,' he said. 'Have another?'

'Thanks, I will.' He's steering clear of them himself, thought Biegler.

'You've seen the charge?' the presiding judge asked him.

'I have, yes.' His mouth was full of flour and sugar.

'Then we can begin. If you don't want a longer extension to study the case, we could open the trial itself next Monday. Another case has been unexpectedly adjourned, so all of a sudden we can fit this one in.'

'That's a little surprising,' said Biegler. 'In fact I haven't prepared yet. Isn't there going to be a review of the case for remand in custody?'

'No, we'd rather go straight to the trial itself, if you have no objection,' said the presiding judge.

'Then are you quashing the arrest warrant for Eschburg?' asked Biegler.

'Why would we do that?' asked the presiding judge.

'Because his confession can't be used in court. The police officer interrogating him threatened him with torture. Surely Frau Landau's memo makes that perfectly clear,' said Biegler. 'Of course we're glad you can bring the case to court so quickly, but I would like him released from custody.'

The presiding judge nodded. 'The question of torture is one of the problems of this case,' he said. He looked at Landau and waited.

'We can clear that up in the course of the trial itself,' said Landau.

She's good, thought Biegler, not at all unsure of herself. He turned to her from his armchair. 'I don't understand why you haven't cleared it up long ago. Although you were present at the time, you filed Eschburg's confession with the charge sheet as if it were nothing out of the ordinary. But all of us know that it can't be used.'

'The court will decide on that,' said Landau.

152

'Don't be silly,' said Biegler.

'This is a serious matter,' said the presiding judge. 'I have been a judge for nearly thirty years, and I've never had a case involving torture before. If that accusation turns out to be true, then of course we won't be using the confession.' The presiding judge's voice sounded harsh. 'However, I agree with Frau Landau. The court will be able to assess the accusation of torture in the context of the trial itself. Before your client makes his statement, Herr Biegler, we will hear what the police officer has to say, and perhaps also Frau Landau herself as a witness. The question is whether your client will repeat his confession.'

'I haven't discussed that with him yet,' said Biegler. 'But I don't think you have a case here at all. You don't have a body. You don't even know who's supposed to have been murdered. I know that, once before, this court tried a case of murder when no body could be found. But in that case, there were witnesses who saw what happened, and hundreds of clues . . . '

'There were even photographs of the body,' said the presiding judge.

'Yes, indeed. But there's nothing of the kind here,' said Biegler.

'That's not true,' said Landau. 'We have the victim's call to the police. In addition we have the sadistic porn films, the handcuffs, whips, autopsy equipment, traces of blood left in the hire car, the torn dress in the dustbin, and so on. Those clues are independent of your client's confession.'

Biegler liked the way Landau was fighting back. I'd do just the same in her place, he thought.

'So far we know only about a single call from an unknown

woman,' said Biegler. 'But we know nothing about the woman herself. It could be a joke. Or an attempt to cast false suspicion on my client. Eschburg is very well known, and like all people in the public eye he's constantly exposed to such nonsense. You can't build anything on that. As for your other so-called clues – it's not forbidden to have any of those items, is it? And the dress: do you really know why it was torn? Or who tore it? Do you seriously think a court will lock a man up for twenty-five years on such evidence?'

'Your client can ask himself our questions,' said Landau.

'Now you really are being ridiculous,' said Biegler.

'The court will assess the evidence as a whole, not individual parts,' said Landau.

'It's interesting that you always know so precisely what the court will do, but—'

'That will do.' The presiding judge interrupted Biegler. 'You don't have to present a plea here.'

'May I smoke?' asked Biegler.

'Certainly not. This is a public building,' said Landau.

'In fact, it's not a public building, we're in my office,' said the presiding judge. 'All the same, no. But you can have another biscuit.'

Biegler shook his head. He already had heartburn.

'I don't want to anticipate the trial, Frau Landau,' said the presiding judge. 'But I'm afraid you ought to look at the files again. The body of evidence is, in reality, thin.'

'Evidence can't yet be purchased in specialist shops,' said Biegler.

'Don't be so arrogant,' said Landau.

'No?' Biegler lost his temper. 'My client has been remanded

in custody for seventeen weeks. You have been investigating the case for months without being able to put anything reasonable forward. You act as if my client's liberty were a can of cat food. Your interrogating officer threatened him with torture. That hasn't appeared in the press, a state of affairs that will now change, my dear Frau Landau. You have exposed Eschburg's private life to public scrutiny. You have ensured that no one will ever buy his pictures again. But you say nothing about the most important feature of these proceedings. And then you sit there with your legs crossed, accusing me of arrogance?'

'Calm down, please, Herr Biegler,' said the presiding judge. 'We don't know how that information became public property.'

'We don't have to know. It came out in the course of investigations, and Frau Landau is responsible for the course of those investigations. At this point in the proceedings, the defendant is under the special protection of the state. But at the moment it looks – never mind which newspaper you read – as if he were guilty without a shadow of doubt. So how do you expect me to calm down? The biased information policy of the public prosecutor's office is outrageous: I have read the entire file of press reports, and there is not a word about the threat of torture. It's beyond my understanding. And then again, if we're talking about omissions: the charge can't be reconstructed. What is this trial aiming at? A murder without a body is a problem that can hardly be resolved for a start. But how about a murder case in which we don't even know who the victim is supposed to be? That's downright absurd,' said Biegler.

The presiding judge smiled. Biegler did not like that.

'Perhaps you won't have to go to the specialist shops for

evidence after all, Frau Landau,' said the presiding judge, smiling again. 'The court has asked the medical experts to look at the bloodstains again. There was just one little detail, probably overlooked inadvertently. Previously, Herr Biegler, your client's DNA was not compared to the DNA of the presumed victim. That's really a standard part of forensic medicine, but it can be forgotten now and then.'

'I don't understand a word of this,' said Biegler. Landau herself was looking at the presiding judge.

'We've had that oversight remedied. Yesterday evening the Forensic Institute sent us the report.' The presiding judge passed copies to Landau and Biegler. 'The identity of the missing woman is at least partly explained. To sum up briefly: the unknown girl is Eschburg's half-sister.'

5

Next morning, the first thing Biegler did was to go to the remand prison. He placed the new report from the Forensic Institute in front of Eschburg.

'Are you surprised to find that she's your half-sister?' asked Biegler.

'I'm only surprised it took the investigators so long to find out,' said Eschburg.

'You're not exactly making things easy for me, Eschburg.'

'Sorry.'

'Don't you want to help me, or is it that you can't? So far I don't even know whether the woman is the child of your mother or your father. The pathologist said he'd need your parents' DNA for that. I'm sure the public prosecutor's office will look at your mother first, if only because that will be easier,' said Biegler.

Eschburg shrugged his shoulders.

Biegler waited for a while, and then took his notebook out of his jacket pocket. 'Right, let's begin with something else. I have another problem,' he said. 'Last time we talked, you told me about your neighbour in Linienstrasse.'

'Senja Finks,' said Eschburg.

'My colleagues have checked up on that,' said Biegler. 'Obviously no one ever lived there. You had no neighbours.'

Now Eschburg did look surprised. 'But we met. On the rooftop in Linienstrasse, in her apartment, in the hospital.'

'Can you remember who else saw the woman? Anyone else?'

'I don't know ... No, when I saw her I was always on my own. But the attack on her ... I ended up in hospital. There must be hospital records.'

'Yes, there are. The police found them in your apartment.' Biegler took a sheet of pale green paper out of his briefcase. 'This is your discharge sheet from the hospital. It says you fell and hit your head. You also had a laceration and trauma to the skull.'

'It was an attack on her.'

'I know, that's what you told me. After that I asked the police to look into it. They know nothing of any such incident.'

'Of course they don't. I didn't go to the police because Frau Finks asked me not to. But wait a moment ... there must be an old rental agreement for the apartment.'

'My colleagues checked that as well. A joint-stock company in Switzerland is entered in the land register as the last owner of the building. You yourself bought the building from that company, which was dissolved after the sale. The trustee in Zürich has no further files on it.'

'Senja Finks always put the rent into my letterbox in cash. It wasn't a large sum; we never talked about contracts.'

Biegler stood up and went to the window. He felt sorry for Eschburg; his client needed help. 'You must understand: there never was any Senja Finks, the apartment was empty.' Biegler was speaking slowly now. 'I phoned your friend Sofia – she never set eyes on the woman either.'

Eschburg shook his head, seeming to cave in on himself. 'Will you still defend me?' he asked.

'I can't really refuse the brief so close to the trial. The court would then insist on my acting for you through the legal aid system. But you must tell me something about your sister now. If the prosecution moves faster than we do, we could lose the case,' said Biegler.

'Yes,' said Eschburg after a while. 'Yes, I'll tell you about her.'

Leaving the remand prison, Biegler took a taxi to the restaurant where he nearly always had lunch. It was run by Lebanese people who made themselves out to be Italian. In spite of the ban on smoking in restaurants, there was a back room with a fireplace where guests could still smoke. Biegler sat there alone; he had agreed to meet Sofia in this back room.

He ordered a plate of spaghetti. Then he called his chambers and asked his secretary to send out the press release he had written the day before to the news agencies and the newspapers and magazines. He knew that the question of torture would soon be under discussion everywhere.

Of course, he thought, torture and the threatening and deception of a defendant occur much more frequently than is ever disclosed in court. There have always been police officers who thought that was the way for them to act. Biegler was grateful to Landau for writing her memo. Without it, he couldn't prove the torture. No court believes a defendant who makes such a claim himself. What he didn't understand, all the same, was why she had allowed the officer to go ahead with his interrogation.

When Sofia entered the restaurant, he stood up and waved to her across the room. Her appearance was as Eschburg had described her. The other diners turned to look at her. She doesn't fit in here, he thought.

Sofia ordered only a tea. They talked about the demonstrations and building sites and tourists in the city. Then Biegler said, as casually as possible, 'Did you know that the woman who has disappeared is Eschburg's half-sister?'

'What?' She almost screamed it.

'Her DNA has been investigated. There's no doubt about it,' he said.

'I didn't even know he had a sister at all,' said Sofia. 'He's always kept me apart from his family.' Only now did she slip off her coat and drape it over the back of her chair. 'What does that mean for the trial?' she asked.

'Murdering your sister is still a crime,' said Biegler, continuing to eat.

Sofia shook her head. Biegler looked up.

'I'm sorry,' he said, 'but this means that the public prosecutor's office is carrying out further investigations. They'll try to find out who the woman is. Or was.'

'Please believe me, Sebastian is not a murderer.'

'That's what all girlfriends and most wives say,' said Biegler.

'Have you ever noticed how he reacts to meeting people? He always stretches his arm right out to keep them away from him. He can't bear to touch them,' said Sofia.

'Hmm, well,' said Biegler. He wondered whether to have a dessert, even though Elly had forbidden it.

'I just don't believe it,' said Sofia.

'Belief is a funny thing. I once had a client who couldn't leave his apartment for seven years. He was afraid of company; he was another who couldn't touch people. But he met a woman through the Internet. Somehow or other he managed to have a child with her. Then he got stranger and stranger. He couldn't eat anything red or green, and he thought the perfume industry was persecuting him. He talked for hours to people who weren't there and lived entirely on oat flakes. Naturally a time came when his girlfriend left him. But she was a nice girl. She visited him every week, did his shopping for him and took care that he didn't neglect himself entirely. Then she made a mistake. She thought he ought to see their child. He strangled her, and after that he washed her hair, filed her fingernails and toenails, and brushed her teeth. He cut her skin thirty-four times with a kitchen knife, and put little pieces of paper in all the cuts. He wrote the same thing on each of them: *crown cork*. The man was arrested on the stairs coming away from her; the baby was still sitting beside its mother in the kitchen, screaming. The neighbours had seen blood on the man's hands and called the police. He remembered nothing about it. All he remembered was touching the banisters. The banisters were the worst thing of all for him. He said they had been so dirty.'

'What did he mean by writing *crown cork*?' asked Sofia.

'No idea,' said Biegler.

Sofia stared at him and shook her head again.

Biegler shrugged and told her what he had learned from

161

Eschburg: his half-sister came from Austria, and the village where Eschburg's father had had his hunting preserves.

'What will you do now?' asked Sofia.

'What will I do? I'll have to go to Austria, of course, back to those absurd mountains, there's nothing else for it. Obviously I can now consider myself Eschburg's errand boy, so to speak. Not a particularly amusing role, if you ask me,' said Biegler.

'Why didn't Sebastian tell you where his sister is now?'

'He thought I'd understand when I was there. A peculiar answer, don't you think?'

'Sounds just like him,' said Sofia.

'I can't stand surprises. Once, on my birthday, my wife Elly—'

'Did he say whether she's still alive?' asked Sofia.

'No.' He liked Sofia; she's a kind woman, he thought. He wanted to say something reassuring. 'But he didn't say he'd killed her, either.' It didn't sound quite the way he had hoped.

'Can I come with you?' she asked. 'I don't want to hang around here waiting, I can't bear it.'

Biegler wondered whether he would find her company a strain. 'Only if you promise not to keep telling me why he isn't the murderer.'

'All the same, Sebastian didn't do it,' said Sofia. 'He couldn't. I know him.'

Biegler shrugged his shoulders again and asked for the bill. They said goodbye out in the street. He went a few steps, then turned back to Sofia and called after her. 'Listen, do you by any chance know a good tree expert?'

'What?' asked Sofia.

'Oh, forget it.'

He got into a taxi and went home.

Elly came back from her practice in the afternoon. Biegler had opened up the garage and was standing in it. He had taken off his jacket and rolled up his shirtsleeves.

'What are you doing?' asked Elly.

'How do we come to have so many measuring tapes?' asked Biegler. He had beads of sweat on his forehead. 'Nine measuring tapes, three hammers, and not a single pair of pliers. That's peculiar.'

He was holding two cardboard boxes.

'As bad as that?' she asked.

He had an oil stain on his waistcoat. Elly pushed a wooden crate full of old rags and cans aside.

'Wait a minute,' he said. He dropped the boxes, took a large white handkerchief out of his trouser pocket and spread it on the bench. She sat down. He stood in front of her, feeling like a boy.

'So what's the matter?' she asked. 'Whenever you start clearing out the garage there's something wrong.'

'I simply don't understand him,' said Biegler.

'Don't understand who?'

'Eschburg. The artist. I don't understand what he's doing.'

Elly lifted a can of dried-up paint out of the wooden crate. 'Do you remember putting that soap-box together for our son?' she asked.

'I do remember how complicated it was,' said Biegler.

'The instructions said that children of twelve and over could put it together,' said Elly.

'I'm still sure that was a printer's error,' said Biegler. 'It wasn't a particularly good soap-box.' He sat down beside her.

'But it was a nice colour,' said Elly.

He looked at her. Even now, twenty-eight years later, he couldn't understand why she had decided to marry him. His clothes were never spotlessly neat and clean. He felt clumsy beside her, awkward and heavy.

'I think I'm getting old, Elly,' he said.

'You were always old,' said Elly. She put the can of paint back again, and wiped her fingers on a corner of his handkerchief.

'And it was better when telephones were still attached to cables,' said Biegler.

'Tell me about this Eschburg,' she said. 'What's wrong?'

'I don't know. The man's accused of murder, he's confessed. He's in remand prison and the press is writing appalling stuff about him. Yet none of that seems to trouble him at all. The police think he's a cold fish. I don't know that it's as simple as that. He has something that protects him from prison.'

'What do you mean?'

'Do you remember the neighbours in our first apartment? The old man who lived all by himself. I went to see him once. He was sitting in his tiny kitchen in a suit and tie. He'd laid the table perfectly: tablecloth, silver cutlery, wine glass, napkin. He was even wearing cufflinks. He sat alone in his kitchen like that every day, although there was no one there to see him. He did it because he wanted to keep up standards. That old man with his cufflinks was like Eschburg. There was something untouchable about him.'

'That's how you look to most people,' said Elly, after a while.

'When you were a young lawyer, a number of people thought you were a snob.'

'A snob?'

'Well, so you are a little bit. On our first date, we went to the theatre, even though you hate the theatre and have no idea what it's about. You just wanted to impress me. In the middle of the play you whispered to me that Oedipus was the first detective in the history of the world – a man investigating himself without knowing it. Then you said we'd all do the same. You were absolutely certain of yourself. Maybe that's it: *certainty*. Anyway, I found that very attractive.'

'Really?' He smiled at her. She still looks like a girl, he thought.

'Don't get any ideas, Biegler,' she said.

6

The following morning, Biegler and Sofia boarded the first flight to Salzburg. Biegler complained of the cramped seats. He was not a battery chicken, he said.

A woman in the seat beside Biegler's ordered curry sausage, pieces of meat swimming in brown sauce, regenerated in a fan oven for fifteen minutes at 150 degrees. The flight attendant put her hand on Biegler's shoulder and asked whether he would like a sweet or a savoury snack. Biegler began losing his temper. The chief cabin steward came and introduced himself as the purser on board this plane. Biegler informed him that the term purser derived from the Christian seafaring tradition, and indicated that such an officer was in charge of provisions for the journey, but no one could really speak of provisions in this airborne cage.

Sofia tried to calm Biegler down. Biegler said the man had begun it.

'Why did you become a lawyer, Herr Biegler?' she asked.

'I'm no good as a musician,' said Biegler.

'Come on, that's not an answer.'

'The other answer is a long story, and I wouldn't like to bore you.'

'You aren't boring me,' said Sofia.

'Well, maybe it's not so complicated after all; a time came when I realized that a man belongs only to himself. Not to any God or any church, not to any state, only to himself. That's his liberty. And that liberty is a fragile thing, sensitive and vulnerable. Only the law can protect it. Do I sound over-emotional?'

'A little,' said Sofia.

'That's what I believe, all the same.'

'And what will you do when this case is over?' asked Sofia.

'Tackle my next brief, of course. Why?' asked Biegler.

'Won't you get tired of it some day? Don't the constant attacks on you in the press bother you?'

'Acting for the defence in court isn't a popularity contest,' said Biegler.

'But don't you sometimes want to branch out? Go into politics, for instance? Well-known lawyers sometimes do that.'

'Go into politics?'

'Yes, the internationally important questions of the day—'

'The more internationally important a question is, the less it interests me,' said Biegler.

In Salzburg they hired a car and arrived in the mountain village two and a half hours later. They stopped outside the Golden Stag on the marketplace. Biegler rang the doorbell. When no one came to open the door they walked round the house. The garden gate was open. Biegler saw a man with a pockmarked face and grey stubble sitting outside the house. He was about to wave when a dog jumped up at him. There was no avoiding the animal. Biegler fell against the posts of the garden fence. Their sharp points dug into his back.

The man with the pockmarked face shouted, 'Down, Rascal.'

The dog took its forepaws off Biegler's shoulders, looked at him and wagged its tail. The man came over. Biegler straightened his clothing.

'Good boy, Rascal, good boy,' said the man. The dog lay down on the ground.

'I wouldn't call Rascal a good boy myself,' said Biegler. His back hurt.

'He likes you,' said the man. 'He usually bites at once.' The man seemed to be expecting a compliment for Rascal in return.

Sofia bent down to pat the dog. 'What breed is he?' she asked. 'He's so pretty.'

'Pretty? You think this dog is pretty? He's a monster,' said Biegler.

'Bernese mountain dog,' said the man. 'The best dog for these parts.'

'We're looking for the landlady,' said Biegler. He still had dog hairs on his face.

'She's inside the inn.'

'We rang the bell,' said Sofia.

'The bell's out of order,' said the man. 'Who are you?'

'Biegler, lawyer, from Berlin. And I'm allergic to dog hair.'

'So?' said the man. He looked Biegler in the face and grinned. Biegler grinned back. They stood like that for a while, until at last the man gave up. 'Wait here.' He went into the inn by the back door, hardly lifting his feet as he walked.

Sofia helped Biegler to pick the hairs from his clothes. The dog leaned against Biegler's legs, wagging his tail. 'He keeps looking at me,' said Biegler.

'He likes you, that's what it is,' said Sofia.

'He has too much hair.'

A few minutes later the pockmarked man re-emerged from the house and waved them inside. They went through the kitchen into the main room. The tables were light oak, the walls panelled with wood. The place smelled of fresh bread and floor polish. A woman came towards them; she was in her early forties, blue-eyed.

'Who are you?' she asked.

'My name is Biegler, and I'm a lawyer,' said Biegler.

'Yes?'

'We're here because of Sebastian von Eschburg.'

The woman turned, looked at the man who was still standing by the door, and raised her chin. He shuffled out of the room. She waited until he had gone.

'Please sit down.' She pointed to a table, but remained standing herself.

'Has anyone from the police been here?' asked Biegler.

'Why the police?' asked the woman.

'Or the press?'

'No, not the press either. For heaven's sake, what's this about? I read about Sebastian's arrest, but what's that to do with me?'

'Excuse me,' said Biegler, 'but could I have some water, please?'

'Of course.' The woman looked at Sofia. 'Would you like something to drink as well?'

'Water too, please,' said Sofia.

The woman went behind the bar and came back with a bottle and three glasses. She poured the water standing, and then sat down with them.

'What has happened?' she asked.

'I'm sorry, but that's what I have to ask you,' said Biegler. 'Sebastian's father is also the father of your daughter, am I right?' He was watching her. Her upper lip trembled slightly, that was all.

'How do you know?' she asked.

Biegler waited. He imagined her life in this village. It couldn't be easy to be a single mother here. A wooden cross hung near the stove. We invented gods because we were lonely, he thought, but even that was no good.

'Yes, you're right,' the woman said after a long pause. Then she began to tell her story. It was like a dam breaking. She told them how she had met Sebastian's father. That had been over twenty years ago, when she was nineteen. Her father, who was the village innkeeper, had bought a new car, a convertible. Sebastian's father had hired the car, and she had gone for a drive with him. He had opened the roof, although it was already autumn.

'He drove so fast,' she said, 'he laughed and fooled around. He had such slender hands, and soft hair almost like a girl's. We went to the lake, we listened to the radio and looked at the water.'

'And then you stopped looking at the water,' said Biegler.

She nodded. She had been very much in love with him, she said. After four years she became pregnant. She hadn't planned it, she said, it just happened. They used to see each other only when he came here to hunt. He didn't want to lose her, but neither could he leave his family.

'That's the way men are,' she said. 'When my belly grew bigger and everyone could see it, he talked of nothing else, he didn't know what to do. He wept and discussed it this way and that, and then wept again. His thoughts were hopelessly entangled.'

That was when he began drinking, she said. Drinking spirits, the hard stuff, here at the inn. She knew drinkers, she knew there was no helping them.

'It was bad enough for me, but I think it was even worse for him. My father took it calmly; he said we could bring the child up here,' she said. 'After a while I stopped going up to the hunting lodge. I thought that was the best thing to do, before it all tore him apart entirely. Perhaps that was wrong; I sometimes think so now. And when my daughter was born I was on my own.'

The woman emptied her glass. She had stopped talking as suddenly as she had begun. Her upper lip was trembling again. Biegler brought his cigarillos out of his pocket.

'May I?' he asked.

She pushed an ashtray across the table. Biegler lit himself a cigarillo. Sofia was going to say something but Biegler shook his head. The woman looked at the floor, and then watched him smoking.

'And then I heard that he had killed himself,' she said at last. 'I didn't know until he was already buried because no one at his home knew about me. People said he'd shot his head away. He never saw his daughter.'

I must go on, thought Biegler. 'But they kept showing your daughter's photograph on TV. Why didn't you get in touch with the police?'

'What photograph?' asked the woman.

Biegler drew the photo that Eschburg had taken out of the file.

The woman took the picture. 'Yes, I've seen that. But who is it of?'

Sofia and Biegler stared at the woman. She's not lying, Biegler reflected. He was furious with himself. He must have over-looked something or other.

'I thought that was your daughter,' he said.

She shook her head. 'I've never seen this girl before.' She looked at the photo again. 'The mouth is a little like my daughter's, but that's all.'

The mouth is like her daughter's, thought Biegler; maybe there's another illegitimate daughter?

'Sebastian is accused of her murder,' said Sofia.

'Good heavens, no,' said the woman. 'Sebastian could never harm anyone.'

'Do you know him?' asked Sofia.

'He's been here a few times. He inherited his father's hunting lodge. His mother wanted to sell it but his father had transferred it to his son for life.'

'Has he ever been here with your daughter?' asked Biegler. He had let his cigarillo go out, something that very seldom happened.

The woman nodded. 'Wait a moment,' she said, and left the room. After a couple of minutes she came back. She was carrying a cardboard box. She put it on the table and opened it. Sofia took out the papers it contained: they were pictures of Eschburg's exhibitions, newspaper cuttings, interviews, critical assessments of his work.

'This belongs to my daughter,' the woman said. 'She collected everything she could find about Sebastian before she saw him for the first time. He meant the right sort of life to her. She was furious with her father, although she never met him. She used to scream and rage and curse everyone here. I can see why. A stranger can't understand what it's like, growing up in a village like this without a father. She always wanted to get away.'

'And then?' asked Biegler.

'She met Sebastian just after her sixteenth birthday. I couldn't dissuade her. She went to the opening of his exhibition in Rome. After that they were here together twice,' said the woman. 'They got on well, they're very like each other. Before she left she said she'd be part of his art for ever now.'

'Before she left? You mean died?' asked Sofia, and Biegler nodded.

'What makes you think that?' asked the woman. She looked at the two of them. 'No, she left to go to Scotland. Sebastian is paying for her to study at a boarding school there – it's called Gordonstoun. She wants to study art history later,' she said.

'What?' Biegler and Sofia exclaimed at the same time.

'When did you last speak to her?' asked Biegler.

'Yesterday,' said the woman.

'Then she's alive?' asked Sofia.

'Of course she's alive.' The woman sat very upright at the table and stared at Sofia and Biegler. 'Has something happened to her? You ask such odd questions.'

'No,' said Biegler. 'Nothing has happened to her.'

'Can you tell me what she meant by saying that about his art, please? My daughter won't say,' said the woman.

'I have no idea,' said Biegler. He straightened his shoulders, and stood up. 'I'm sorry we had to ask all those things,' he said. Then he went out into the garden.

7

Biegler and Sofia spent the night in the inn's two guest rooms. Biegler slept poorly. He woke twice and didn't know where he was. At five he got up, thinking that he would read, but the only available book was a Bible in the drawer of the bedside table.

He dressed and went out into the marketplace. The coat he had brought was only a thin one. There was mist everywhere, and he could hardly make anything out. He walked through the village and turned, but he had lost his way back to the Golden Stag. All the houses looked the same. He wanted a cigarillo, but his lighter wasn't working. He heard a tractor and had to swerve aside, dazzled by its headlights at the last minute. The tractor driver swore and tapped his forehead. Then he heard a baby being tortured somewhere. He ran in the direction of the screams, stumbled over a doorstep, slipped and hit his shoulder hard on the wall of a house. The screams came from a cat that was sitting on a windowsill, spitting at him. Biegler cursed. Cold sweat stood out on his forehead and his shoulder hurt.

At last he found the entrance to the inn again. All was still dark inside. He sat on the bed in his coat until seven. Then he heard Sofia in the corridor.

They drank coffee in the main room of the inn. Biegler told the landlady that they would like to see the Eschburgs' hunting lodge. The key used to be kept under a stone on the steps outside it, she said, but she hadn't been back there since her daughter's birth. Biegler wanted to pay their overnight bill, but the woman wouldn't take any money.

Sofia and Biegler drove along a narrow path through the fields up to the hunting lodge.

'Who can the girl in that photo be?' Biegler wondered aloud. 'The girl who disappeared. Who called the police?'

'Sebastian's father must have had another child as well,' said Sofia.

'Do you really think so?'

'No,' said Sofia.

'Nor do I,' said Biegler. 'We're no further on at all.'

'Suppose you asked mother and daughter to give evidence in court?'

'Their blood would be tested. If their DNA matches the traces of blood that have been found, the verdict would probably be not guilty, although nothing else would be cleared up.'

'And if it doesn't?' asked Sofia.

'Then we'd be facing the same problem again. I'll do it if necessary: I'll ask them both to give evidence. But I don't like the idea. You don't ask questions in court unless you already know the answer,' said Biegler.

*

It had begun to rain. They found the key under a stone on the step outside the front door. The door itself was jammed. Once inside the house they discovered that the electricity was turned off and the shutters over the windows were closed. Biegler crashed into a chair in the front hall. He found the handle of a window and opened it. The catch for the shutters was rusty and Biegler cut his hand on it. He wrapped his handkerchief round the injury. They went through the rooms, opening all the windows one by one.

'This is terrible,' said Sofia.

Eschburg's father had drawn them straight on the walls. There must be hundreds of thousands of them, all over the entire hunting lodge: crosses had been drawn on every wall, on the ceilings, the chairs, the tables, the cupboards. The crosses were tiny and black, two strokes of fine charcoal to each. It must have taken him weeks.

After they had seen everything, they went outside the door and sat down on the wooden bench under the porch. For a long time they sat there, listening to rain falling on the porch roof.

'It reminds me of Goya, Herr Biegler. He did the same thing. He painted his nightmares on the walls of his country house; they're known as the Black Paintings. Subjects like giants eating human beings, biting their heads off. They're perhaps the best pictures he ever created.'

Sofia's lips were blue. Biegler took off his coat and draped it over her shoulders. 'Does anyone know why?' he asked.

'Goya had gone deaf; he was living in a world of his own. I think it was because of his isolation, the loss of his hearing.'

Biegler nodded. 'I'm glad you came with me,' he said.

He lit a cigarillo but didn't like the taste of it. 'Did you know that given the chance, most suicides shoot themselves in the head? Not in the heart, in the head. It's the horror they feel for themselves. We can't bear our own guilt. We can manage to forgive anyone else, our enemies, those who deceive us, people who let us down. It's only with ourselves it doesn't work. We simply can't forgive ourselves. We ourselves are the stumbling block.'

'And yet,' said Sofia, after a while, 'the woman loved him.'

'That didn't save him,' said Biegler. He stretched out his legs. The Bernese mountain dog had left paw prints on his trousers.

'People can change,' said Sofia.

'Oh, come on, that's the kind of thing that characters played by James Stewart say in films. No, people don't change except in novels. We stand side by side, we hardly touch at all. There's no development. Things happen to us, maybe they turn out well, mostly they don't. We learn to hide who we really are,' said Biegler.

Sofia pulled Biegler's coat closer around herself. 'Perhaps Sebastian knew his father's story, and the story of Goya's Black Paintings. Perhaps that's why he created that photo of *The Maja's Men*,' she said.

'Perhaps. When did you and he separate?' asked Biegler.

'Soon after he met her. I didn't know she was his sister. He said he had to be alone. Then he phoned me in Paris, only a day before he was arrested, eleven months after we separated, eleven months when I almost went crazy. He said he needed me. I went to Berlin at once, but he was already under arrest. I've been visiting him in remand prison every two weeks. We haven't talked about the case because he didn't want to.' She put her hand on Biegler's arm. 'I miss him so much. It feels as if someone has drawn the curtains and put out the light. What's the point of it all?'

'Most questions remain open-ended.' Biegler looked at the time. 'You haven't had enough sleep. Do sit in the car, it'll be warmer there,' he said.

He went back into the house, closed the shutters and locked the door. Down in the village, he could indistinctly make out the roof of the inn.

8

The trial was to begin at nine a.m. Journalists and cameramen were standing outside the courthouse, and inside the building the corridors and the courtroom where the trial was to be held were also crowded. Biegler had never seen so many reporters concentrating on a case before. The day before, two large television news channels had announced that they would be covering the trial. He saw Monika Landau, as counsel for the prosecution, surrounded by microphones, but in such a throng he couldn't hear what she was saying. Before the trial, he had given almost every newspaper an interview on the subject of torture; he had even appeared on a talk show, much as he disliked that kind of thing. Now, when he entered the courtroom, the presiding judge was leaning against the judges' bench and talking to the woman who, as court reporter, would be keeping the minutes for his records. He nodded to Biegler.

'Looks like being a strenuous day,' said the presiding judge.

Biegler brushed this aside. 'A lot of fuss,' he said.

A few minutes after Biegler had taken his seat, a small door in the wooden panelling opened and two police officers brought Eschburg into the courtroom. He sat down next to Biegler, looking composed.

It was almost thirty minutes before the journalists and spectators had taken their places. The police officers had to ask for quiet several times. When the professional judges and the lay judges who assisted them entered the room, the lawyers acting in the trial and the spectators stood up.

'This session of the 14th Criminal Court is now open,' said the presiding judge. 'Sit down, please.'

The presiding judge then established the presence of those taking part in the trial. Then he asked Eschburg his name, date of birth and last place of residence.

'If there are no petitions, I will ask the representative of the Public Prosecutor's Office to read out the arraignment,' said the presiding judge.

As almost always in such major trials, the arraignment was short: Eschburg was accused of abducting and murdering his half-sister. Her body had not been found, and in view of these special circumstances no features of the murder could be established.

Public Prosecutor Landau was wearing a white blouse and a white scarf under her robe. She's a pretty woman, Biegler reflected, and was then annoyed with himself for letting this inappropriate thought cross his mind.

The presiding judge explained that the district court had allowed the charge to go straight to the main trial. Then he turned to Eschburg, and instructed him in his right to remain silent. So far, it was all routine; matters were running as in any other trial for murder.

'We now,' said the presiding judge, 'have an unusual situation. In principle it is the defendant's right to express an opinion on the charges at once. In this trial, however, there is another factor, to the effect that before the defendant made a confession he was threatened with torture by a police officer. Should that turn out to be true, his confession could not be used in court. The defendant could then decide, again, how to act: whether to remain silent or make a statement. The court has therefore decided to hear what the police officer concerned has to say before any subsequent statement may be made by the defendant. Are those concerned with the progress of these proceedings in agreement, or are there any objections?'

Biegler and Landau nodded. At the mention of torture, the spectators on their allotted benches had become restless. The journalists had placed notepads on their knees and were making notes.

The police officer who had interrogated Eschburg wore a suit and tie. The presiding judge asked him the usual questions: how old he was, where he lived, whether he was related to the defendant. He answered fast, as if it were routine. He was used to speaking in a law court. The presiding judge reminded the police officer that he must tell the truth. The officer nodded.

'I will now make the content of Public Prosecutor Landau's memo known. It is on page 105 of the fourth volume of the files.' The presiding judge waited until the court recorder had written that down. Then he said, 'According to that memo, you are said to have threatened the defendant in the course of an interrogation. You are said to have called him a bastard and a rapist, and to have threatened him with torture. The defendant then confessed to a crime. He said he had killed the young woman and disposed of her body. The confession is not complete because at that point Public Prosecutor Landau interrupted the interrogation. So much for the memo.'

The presiding judge leaned slightly forward and looked directly at the police officer.

'I would now like to hear the witness's account of the course of this interrogation. Before you say anything, however, I must point out that you may refuse to answer any such questions if by doing so you expose yourself to the risk of prosecution. In that case, you may remain silent. But if you do say anything, it must be the truth.'

The presiding judge turned to the court recorder. 'Instruction given in accordance with Clause 55, Code of Criminal Procedure,' he dictated to her, before going on.

'It is also my opinion that you may even remain silent on *any* question concerning the interrogation, when you could have made yourself liable to prosecution for coercion, bodily harm and other offences. So you do not even have to say that you interrogated the defendant.'

'The law protects you,' said Biegler out loud.

'Please do not interrupt me, Herr Biegler,' said the presiding judge. He turned to the police officer again. 'Public Prosecutor Landau has told the court that preliminary proceedings against you have been instituted. You can also call on a lawyer of your choice to assist you in any evidence you give as a witness concerning this interrogation. Do you fully understand all that?'

The police officer nodded.

'How do you choose to proceed?' asked the presiding judge.

'I will decline to make any statement,' said the police officer. His voice was firm.

Public Prosecutor Landau looked up from her files.

Of course he's taken advice, thought Biegler. There were only two possible strategies in such a situation: denial or silence. Denial was no longer possible.

'Then I have no questions for the witness,' said the presiding judge. 'Does anyone else involved in these proceedings have a question for the witness, or can he be discharged?'

Public Prosecutor Landau shook her head.

'I have a few questions for the witness,' said Biegler. Once again, the spectators became restless.

'Quiet, please,' said the presiding judge. He turned to Biegler. He sounded impatient, almost cynical. 'Of course, Herr Biegler, I was sure that, as counsel for the defence, you would have questions. Go ahead.'

Biegler did not react to the implied reproach. He had accepted the brief in order to clear up this one point, and he must at least try. 'How long have you been in the police force?' he asked.

'Thirty-six years,' said the officer.

'And when did you join the murder squad?'

'Twelve years ago.'

'How many cases of murder have you investigated in that time?' Biegler had encountered the police officer in many previous trials; he was a man who knew his job.

'I don't remember precisely, but a great many,' said the officer.

'In all the time you have been in the police force, that is to say the last thirty-six years, how often have preliminary proceedings against you been instituted?'

'Never before.'

'So you have never been accused of menaces, coercion, bodily harm or any other indictable offence?'

'This is the first time.' The police officer glanced briefly at Landau, who was impassive.

'So you could be described as a very experienced officer who knows the law and has never before been at odds with it?'

'I could.'

'You gave an interview to a tabloid newspaper shortly before this trial opened. Wait a moment, please.' Biegler leafed through the file lying on the desk in front of him. 'Here we are.' He held up a sheet of newsprint.

'I haven't seen this interview,' said Landau.

'Then get hold of it,' said Biegler, 'and don't interrupt me again.'

He turned back to the police officer. 'You are reported as having said, in your interview, the following – I quote: "Imagine that a terrorist hides a nuclear bomb somewhere in Berlin, and it is timed to go off in an hour's time. We have found the terrorist, but we don't know where his bomb is. I have to make a decision. Do I torture him, and save four million lives? Or do I fold my hands in my lap and do nothing?" Is it true that you said that?'

'I wouldn't like to say.'

'Why not? Because you might incriminate yourself?' asked Biegler.

'The witness can refuse to answer that question too,' said Landau.

'Really?' asked Biegler. 'Are you no longer willing to stand by what you said to a newspaper with a circulation of millions? For fear of criminal prosecution? Like the criminals whom you usually investigate?'

'Your honour,' said Landau, addressing the presiding judge, 'I move that defending counsel be requested to keep quiet. He is putting pressure on the witness.'

'The witness is experienced enough to decide for himself,' said the presiding judge. 'I've instructed him in his rights. He knows that he doesn't have to answer.'

Biegler was still looking at the police officer, who turned in his chair to return his gaze. Getting somewhere at last, thought Biegler.

'Once again, won't you tell us something about that interview? This has nothing to do with your interrogation of the defendant, it's solely a question of your attitude.'

The police officer undid both buttons of his suit jacket. 'Very well,' he said. He exhaled audibly. 'I would make sure I got terrorists to talk. Even by means of torture, if nothing else worked. My job is to protect citizens. I stand by that.'

A spectator applauded. The presiding judge looked at him. 'If you do that again I will have you removed from the courtroom,' he said.

'And what,' Biegler went on, 'would you do if your prisoner still refuses to say anything? He's a terrorist, remember, he's been trained to withstand torture. He's laughing at you. Now, you happen to know that the man has a fourteen-year-old daughter. You are sure that he'll talk if you torture his daughter before his eyes. Would you do that, too?'

'No, I wouldn't. The daughter is innocent.'

'But so are all the other people in this city,' said Biegler. 'You could save four million of those innocent lives. A little torture against the safety of the whole of Berlin. That's more like a fair deal, surely.'

'I . . .'

'So, to your way of thinking: the girl can't help what her father is like. She is innocent, you tell yourself, I must not torture her.'

'That's right,' said the police officer.

'Then the innocent must never be tortured?'

'That's how I see it.'

'But how about your terrorist? How do you know that he's guilty? Just like that? On the grounds of evidence? Your gut feeling?' asked Biegler.

'It was only an example,' said the police officer.

'An example for first-year law students. But I am asking you as an experienced police officer. Do you think a terrorist would walk into the police station and say: hi, how are you? By the way, I've just hidden a little nuclear bomb in Berlin, timed to go off in an hour from now, but I'm not saying where it is.'

'That's ridiculous,' said the officer. 'In my example we'd have been keeping the terrorist under observation for months. We'd know he was a terrorist, we'd know he was guilty.'

'Guilt established by observation. I see. And how would you know he's hidden a bomb? Have you observed that as well? If so, how come you didn't arrest him on the spot? Why didn't you keep tabs on his mobile phone? Why don't you know who his contacts are? Why haven't you evaluated the contents of his laptop? In other words: isn't it always the case that there's much more going on than the mere information that a terrorist has hidden a ticking bomb?' asked Biegler.

'The example was only intended to show what an exceptional situation we could be in,' said the police officer. 'I meant to explain how it can be necessary to adopt harsh measures.'

'But you would admit that no such case really exists.'

'As I said, it's only an example,' said the police officer.

'Right. Then, if I understand you correctly, you would torture the terrorist to get the truth out of him.'

'So that the bomb could be defused,' said the officer.

'Do you believe that all witches have slept with the Devil?' asked Biegler.

'What?'

'I mean, are you aware that one reason why torture has come to be considered wrong is because prisoners in pain will confess to anything? They don't tell the truth, they say whatever the torturer wants to hear. During the Inquisition all witches slept with the Devil – or at least, that's what they said if they were tortured for long enough. A time came when even the Pope realized it was useless as a means of getting at the truth. In your example of the ticking bomb, you can't check whether the terrorist is telling the truth in time.'

'Maybe not. But maybe I can find the bomb and defuse it.'

'So you would use torture if, *maybe*, it would help?'

'I . . . I'd have to do it to save human lives.'

'I understand,' said Biegler.

'And in my example we know that he's hidden the bomb,' said the officer.

'That's the wonderful thing about your example. You know

everything. Including the fact that he'll tell the truth under torture ... You said that, as an experienced member of the police force, you were familiar with the law.'

'Yes.'

'And with the constitution of this country?'

'Of course,' said the officer.

'So you know that everyone – even an abductor – is under the protection of that constitution. Is it clear to you that by torturing prisoners, you are infringing their constitutional rights?'

'And what about the constitutional rights of the victim of a crime?' asked the officer.

'I think I see what you mean,' said Biegler. 'You make a decision. You tell yourself, for instance, that an abducted child is innocent, the abductor is guilty. He has forfeited his constitutional rights, and I may therefore torture him.'

'To save the child. It would be torture for a good end,' said the officer.

'Torture for a good end?' said Biegler. 'Then it is simply a kind of extra harsh interrogation with a noble aim in mind?'

'Yes.'

'Perhaps under medical supervision?'

'I can envisage that, yes,' said the police officer.

'Long after torture was abolished in this country, the Nazis reintroduced it. They too thought up a special expression for it. Do you know what it was?'

'No.'

'They called it "aggravated methods of interrogation". Sounds almost as nice as "torture for a good end", don't you think? But let's return to our example. By what means will you come to your decision?'

'Which decision?' asked the police officer.

'You have to decide whom to torture,' said Biegler.

'I told you already: the child is innocent, the abductor is guilty,' said the officer.

'So you would torture anyone who's guilty?'

'No, only in extreme circumstances, of course,' said the officer.

'Imagine the abductor tells you, "Yes, I did kidnap the girl. But she is in a nice house, she has plenty of food and warmth, she has enough books to read and games to play." Then what? Do you torture the abductor in those circumstances?'

'I ... I ...'

'I mean,' said Biegler, 'where do you draw the line? When may you torture someone? Only when a girl of ten has been abducted? Or maybe when the victim is a homeless man of fifty, a social near-outcast? You'd do it if the President of the Federal Republic was abducted? But if it's a man known to be a rapist, you'd rather not? Who, in your world, decides when torture may be inflicted? You yourself? As a kind of judge, public prosecutor, counsel for the defence and executioner all rolled into one?'

'That's enough,' said Public Prosecutor Landau.

'I protest,' said Biegler. 'This is the second time. If you want the court to forbid me to speak, apply in due form. We're conducting a trial for murder, not taking part in a talk show when anyone can say what he likes. At the moment I have the right to speak, and you should keep silent.' He got control of himself again, and said more quietly, 'Let's please try to understand the witness.'

'I'll allow defence counsel's question,' said the presiding judge. 'I'm interested myself.'

The policeman considered briefly. Then he said, 'I'm not a qualified lawyer.'

'This isn't a question of legal qualifications,' said Biegler.

'I'd ask a specialist, for instance an investigating magistrate,' said the police officer.

'That's always a good answer. But then why, in our present case, didn't you ask an investigating magistrate whether torture was justified?'

'It would have taken much too long,' he said.

'Nonsense. You could have made a decision like that within ten minutes,' said Biegler. 'I can tell you why you didn't ask an investigating magistrate: you knew what the answer would be. The idea would have been thrown out at once. No, you wanted to make the decision all by yourself. You wanted to judge the defendant.'

The police officer flushed red. He said in a loud voice, 'Oh, did I? It's all very well for you to sit here in a warm courtroom, talking about constitutional rights. But in the police we're on the sharp end. We're there to protect your life and the lives of your family. You call us in when things look dangerous, and then we're supposed to deal with it. But in here you have the nerve to compare me with the Nazis. Think again: suppose I could have saved that young woman's life?' He stared at Biegler, his mouth hanging open.

This is a good man, thought Biegler. He's doing everything wrong, but I would indeed entrust my family to him. Biegler waited. It was quiet in the courtroom; even the on-duty policeman had stopped tipping his chair back and forth. Then he said, softly, 'I'm a lawyer, I don't answer questions, I ask them. That's the way the rules of the courtroom have it. But I can make an exception, if the court will allow me.'

The presiding judge nodded.

'If you'd saved the young woman you would have been a hero,' said Biegler.

'A hero?' The police officer sounded shaken.

Biegler went on, his voice lower now. 'Yes, a tragic hero. You've set yourself against our legal system and all that I believe in. You've transgressed a man's constitutional rights, something that no one can either acquire or lose, but the torture you inflict makes a human being a mere object, there only for you to get something out of him. So if it was all up to me, you'd have to be severely punished for what you did. I'd withdraw your pension and dismiss you from the police force. But I would admire you for sacrificing your future to save the young woman's life. For you, the consequences would certainly be terrible. Heroes are admired, but they perish.'

'And how else would I get a confession? What's the best method of interrogation?' The policeman had lowered his voice too, and was looking at the witness's desk in front of him.

'Courtesy,' said Biegler. 'Ask anyone who's been a prisoner of war. He'll never talk about physical torment, he'll describe the isolation, the sense of abandonment. He wants someone to talk to him as a human being.'

'And suppose I don't get any answers?' asked the police officer.

'Then you don't,' said Biegler.

The police officer raised his head and looked at Biegler. 'You may be right,' he said. 'All the same, I'd do it again.'

The courtroom was growing noisy once more. Many questions are better never asked, thought Biegler.

The officer put his hand to the neck of his shirt and loosened his tie. Biegler saw that his shirt collar was damp with sweat.

'Are there any more questions for the witness? No? Then you are discharged. Thank you very much.'

The police officer got to his feet, shaking his head, and left the courtroom.

'Well,' said the presiding judge, 'now we must consider the matter of the inadmissibility of the confession. We shall need time for that. We will meet here again at nine a.m. on Thursday. Those most closely concerned in the trial have already been informed. The trial is adjourned.'

'Thank you,' said Eschburg to Biegler, when they were alone.

'It's not over yet. Next time the presiding judge will ask you whether you want to make a statement. We'd better discuss that in the remand prison this afternoon. But above all we must ask your sister to come here now,' said Biegler.

'No,' said Eschburg, shaking his head. He gave Biegler a folded note. 'Will you go to this address? You'll be given an envelope. Look at everything in it, and then please come back to me. There's the only statement I'm going to make at this trial. We don't need my sister.'

Biegler took the note and unfolded it. 'This is the address of a notary,' he said.

Eschburg nodded.

'Another job for your errand boy?' asked Biegler.

Eschburg smiled.

'Don't go too far, Eschburg,' said Biegler. He left the court-room. In the corridor, he answered the journalists' questions. But all the time he was thinking of the note in his pocket.

9

Leaving the courthouse, Biegler went straight to the address that Eschburg had given him. The notary greeted him in friendly tones; they knew each other from their student days. He gave Biegler a large sealed envelope and wished him luck.

Still in the street, Biegler tore the envelope open at once. It contained only a USB stick and a document. He took a taxi to his chambers and put the memory stick in his laptop. Half an hour later Biegler's secretary came into his office. She saw him sitting at his open laptop – and smiling, not at all like his usual self.

Biegler asked his secretary to go out, buy a large television set and have it sent to the courthouse. He phoned the presiding judge and explained that Eschburg needed the screen for the statement he would be making in court. After some discussion, the presiding judge agreed to allow it and asked Biegler to inform Public Prosecutor Landau.

Biegler went to the courthouse, bought two coffees from the vending machine, and made his way to Public Prosecutor Landau's office.

'I've brought us two plastic mugs of coffee,' he said.

'Sounds delicious,' she said.

'You can leave out the sarcasm,' Biegler replied. He sat down on her visitor's chair, slopping coffee from the mug on the sleeve of his jacket.

'Don't worry, it'll come out,' she said. 'Plain water will do it.'

'Good,' he said.

'Just don't rub it into the fabric.'

They sat in silence. Biegler knew what was coming now, and felt uncomfortable about it.

'I was impressed by your questioning of the police officer,' said Landau.

'No need for that,' said Biegler.

'No, really, I made a mistake,' she said. 'I shouldn't have left him alone with your client.' She spoke quietly.

'That's all right. I've had a word with the presiding judge. After what the officer said, the court will assume that your memo is correct, so the presiding judge won't call you as a witness.'

'Thank you,' said Landau. She seemed relieved. 'Good – and what is your client going to say when the trial resumes?'

'Let it come as a surprise,' said Biegler.

'You make a theatrical production out of everything,' said Landau.

'To some extent you may even be right. But that's because every trial is theatrical, don't you think?' said Biegler. 'We re-enact the crime with words, petitions, witnesses, evidence. Our forefathers thought that if we did so, evil would lose its power over us. It wasn't such a stupid idea.'

'I still think Eschburg killed the woman,' said Landau. 'There can't be any other explanation.'

'There's always another explanation,' said Biegler.

'You're fooling yourself, Herr Biegler.'

'Am I? And if I am, why not?' replied Biegler.

'Why not? Because of course it's never good to fool yourself.'

'Nonsense,' said Biegler. 'When I go to bed I pretend I'm asleep until I really do fall asleep.'

Landau laughed. 'But seriously, Herr Biegler: aren't you at all afraid?'

'What do you mean?' asked Biegler.

'Suppose your client's confession is the truth? Suppose the police officer was right after all?'

'He messed it up. The rest of the evidence isn't enough on its own,' said Biegler. 'It's as simple as that. End of story.'

'How can you be so cold?' asked Landau.

'Is that what you really think?' said Biegler.

'Yes, I do.'

Biegler closed his eyes. 'It's not about whether or not I'm cold, or about the criminals with whom we concern ourselves every day here. It's only about you and me and the judges doing our job properly. If you still don't understand that then you're in the wrong job.'

Landau flushed red, and did not reply.

'Eschburg will explain himself when the trial resumes,' said Biegler. 'He needs a television set for that, so we've bought a flat-screen TV to be installed in the courtroom. The presiding judge has agreed. I just wanted to let you know.' He got to his feet.

He shook hands with her; he had not meant to sound so abrupt. 'You know, with every new case I think that this time, for once, I may do everything right. But it never works. See you tomorrow, then.'

'See you tomorrow,' said Landau.

He went down the wide staircase to the exit. The policeman on duty greeted him and wished him a nice evening. Biegler wished him the same. He saw his own blurred reflection in the glass panes of the old doors: a man who was rather too stout, carrying a briefcase and wearing a hat.

He took a taxi to Savignyplatz, went into his favourite café, ordered a double espresso to take outside and sat down where he could smoke. He put his briefcase on his knees. A photographic exhibition was announced on the advertising pillar near the café: *Twentieth-Century European Photography*. The poster showed a naked woman against a dark background. Biegler closed his eyes.

Suddenly he said, out loud, 'I'm an idiot.' In fact he said it *too* loud; other customers turned to look at him.

He searched for his mobile phone and called his secretary. 'You once showed me how your computer can translate things as well,' he said. He had to wait a moment for his secretary to bring up the page. 'Please would you see if the Ukrainian word *Finks* means anything in German.' He could hear her typing it in.

'No, there's nothing.'

'Try *Senja Finks*.'

'Still nothing.'

'I always knew the Internet was useless. Stay on the line,

please,' said Biegler. Wedging the phone between his shoulder and his ear, he took his notebook out of his coat pocket, opened it and scribbled in pencil. 'Try typing just the initial of the first name and then the surname. Try it like that, SFINKS.' Biegler spelled out the name.

'Oh, here we are − a hit. The translation is *Sphinx*. Wait a moment, here's the definition: "the Sphinx is a woman with the body of a winged lion who devours everyone who cannot solve her riddle".'

'I know who she is,' said Biegler, and hung up.

He finished his coffee, got to his feet and paid. Out on the pavement he hummed Oscar Peterson's 'On a Clear Day'. Then he stopped abruptly and set his briefcase down on the ground. He moved his legs, turned his toes, held his arms at an angle and performed four or five steps of the twist. Konrad Biegler was dancing.

10

'Good morning, ladies and gentlemen,' said the presiding judge. 'This session of the 14th Criminal Court of the regional court is resumed. We will continue with the trial.' The presiding judge looked in turn at Eschburg, Biegler and Landau.

'Has any more been discovered about the defendant's half-sister?' he asked.

Public Prosecutor Landau cleared her throat. 'I have a report here from the criminal investigation department in Freiburg. According to the civil register, the defendant's mother was married twice. There was only one child of her first marriage, the defendant himself. Her second marriage was childless. Today the defendant's mother is paraplegic – she had a riding accident four years ago.'

'Then the defendant's half-sister is his father's child,' said the presiding judge.

'Yes,' said Landau.

'And?' asked the presiding judge.

'We haven't been able to find out any more,' said Landau.

'Do we have any other evidence so far unknown to us?' asked the presiding judge.

Landau shook her head.

'Or any other trails to be investigated?' asked the presiding judge.

'No, we have no more leads.'

'Herr Biegler? Do you have anything to say?' asked the presiding judge.

Biegler shook his own head in turn.

'Then I will announce the following as the decision of the court: no use can be made of the defendant's confession.'

There was uproar on the spectators' benches. One man shouted, 'Murderer!' The presiding judge had him removed from the courtroom. Then he read out the reasons for the court's decision. The investigating police officer's conduct was understandable in human terms, he said, but the code of criminal procedure recognized only one consequence of his offence: the defendant's confession could not be used, and Eschburg was now in the position of someone who had never confessed to a crime. The decision was a long document; the judges had written it with the appeal court in mind, and wanted to make their case watertight. When the presiding judge had finished, he looked at Eschburg.

'Have you understood our decision?' asked the presiding judge. 'Is there anything you want to discuss with your defence counsel?'

'I understood it all,' said Eschburg.

'Good. Then I will also inform you that you do not have to make any statement here. Your earlier confession will not be taken into account. If you remain silent, that silence cannot be used against you either. Do you understand?'

'I do,' said Eschburg.

The presiding judge turned to the court reporter. 'Please make a note that the defendant was informed of this in a qualified sense.' He turned to Biegler. 'If I have understood you correctly, your client would like to make a statement today.'

Biegler nodded.

'Go ahead,' said the presiding judge.

Eschburg stood up.

'You can remain seated,' said the presiding judge.

'Thank you, I'd rather stand.' Eschburg adjusted the microphone in front of him. Then he took a sheet of paper out of the inner pocket of his jacket and began to read aloud from it.

'In 1770, Baron Wolfgang von Kempelen demonstrated a remarkable machine to the Empress of Austria. It consisted of a wooden figure the size of a man sitting at a chessboard. Under the board there was a chest containing a mechanism of cogwheels, rollers, pulleys, slides and cylinders. The wooden figure was dressed as a Turk. Guests to the show could challenge the chess-playing Turk to a match. Before any game, the baron wound up the machine with a key. Then the mechanical Turk moved the pieces on the board with his wooden arm. He won almost every game. The baron travelled all over Europe with him. The mechanical Turk became famous: the automaton played against the greatest masters of the time. Scientists tried to understand his mechanism. Books were written about him, memorandums, newspaper articles, lectures. No one could understand how he functioned. Even Napoleon and Benjamin Franklin lost to him. Edgar Allan Poe wrote about him, and so, at a later date, did a president of West Germany. The automaton fell victim to a fire in a Philadelphia museum in 1854.'

Eschburg paused for a moment. He sipped a little water. The

judges and the public prosecutor were looking at him. Total silence reigned in the courtroom. Biegler was leaning back with his hands folded over his paunch and his eyes closed.

'Of course, the mechanical Turk was only a trick. No mechanism of the time could really have played chess. There was a man wedged in the chest with the mechanical apparatus, and he played the games. However, the special feature was not the Turk who played chess; the unusual thing about it all was Wolfgang von Kempelen himself. He was not a fraud, but a gifted scientist, an educated man and a high-ranking civil servant. He was in charge of Austrian salt production in the Banat area, he wrote plays and draughted engravings of landscapes. Later he invented an early typewriter for the blind, and an apparatus that could speak entire sentences. Whenever new theories about the functioning of the mechanical Turk were propounded, Kempelen would frankly say that it was based on deception. But that was not what people wanted to hear.'

Eschburg placed his sheet of paper on the table. He gazed straight at his judges, and then sat down again.

Biegler handed the text to the presiding judge.

'Is that your explanation?' the presiding judge asked Eschburg. His voice was a little hoarse.

'Yes,' said Eschburg.

'And this is your signature?'

Eschburg nodded.

'Then we will add the explanation to the records of the trial.' The presiding judge gave the sheet of paper to the court reporter. Then he turned to Eschburg. 'I haven't discussed what I am about to say with anyone in this court. All the same,

I would like you to know that I don't understand. You have been accused of murder, you spent over four months in remand prison, and now you tell us something about a *chess-playing automaton?*'

'I did say earlier that my client won't answer questions,' remarked Biegler, without changing his attitude or opening his eyes. 'Maybe it would help if you thought a little about the explanation.'

Landau appeared furious. 'That is not a useful comment on the charge of murder.'

'Oh, yes, it is,' said Biegler, and he opened his eyes. 'If I may add a little detail: in German, we have the expression *to be Turked*, meaning to be deceived or taken in, and it derives from von Kempelen's chess-playing automaton.'

The presiding judge raised his hand and looked at Eschburg again. 'You have an experienced defence counsel, Herr von Eschburg. I'm sure you have discussed this with him. All the same, I don't understand what you are saying.' He waited for a moment. Eschburg did not react. The presiding judge shrugged and turned to Biegler. 'So that's it: no questions to the defendant?'

'That's it,' said Biegler.

'Are there any other statements or explanations?' asked the presiding judge.

'Yes,' said Biegler. He leaned forward. 'The second part of the explanation is a video. With the permission of the court, we will show it now.'

The two policemen on duty drew the yellow curtains in the courtroom, plunging it into semi-darkness. Using a remote control, Biegler switched on the large screen. The television set was so far behind the judges' bench that everyone in the court-room could see it.

It was a computer-animated film. The mechanical Turk appeared on the screen. He was moving his arm as he played against an invisible opponent. Now the Turk was playing faster and faster, sweeping the chessmen off the board. In the end the only pieces left were the black king, two black rooks and a white pawn. Those pieces now appeared on the screen in close-up. The black king and the two rooks were wearing judges' robes. They looked down at the white pawn. The pawn bowed and then became fluid, turning into a white substance that ran over the chessboard and trickled down into the automaton.

A door under the mechanical Turk opened. A naked young woman climbed out from between the cylinders and cog-wheels in the chest; she was the same colour as the fluid that had been the pawn. She stood with her back to the camera and slowly turned round. Hundreds of small black crosses were drawn on her skin. The camera zoomed in on her face. It was the face of Eschburg's half-sister.

To left and right, two more faces emerged from the darkness: the faces of Eschburg and Sofia. All three faces were the same size and shown in the same light. A scalpel appeared, cutting out the parts of the images showing Sofia's eyes and Eschburg's nose. Both parts were moved to fit above the half-sister's face; only her mouth remained the same. A large eraser smoothed out the joins. The new face was made up of the faces of Sofia, Eschburg and his sister – and everyone in the courtroom rec-ognized it. It was the photograph that had been found everywhere in Eschburg's studio when it was searched – the woman the police had been looking for.

The woman with the new face turned and went over to the mechanical Turk. She had a gun in her hand. She aimed it at the figure's head. The camera followed the shot cartridge; the head exploded into thousands of tiny balls. They were dark green and formed into a line of text:

Down the rivers of the windfall light

After that, the television set turned itself off.

There was commotion on the spectators' benches. Some of the journalists were hurrying out to call their editorial offices. The police officers on duty opened the curtains again. The presiding judge tried several times to restore peace and quiet in the courtroom, and then told one of the officers to make a note of the names of those responsible for the disturbance.

When it was finally calm again, Biegler stood up. 'Your honour,' he addressed the presiding judge, 'at the same time as that film was being shown in this courtroom it also went out on all available video platforms on the Internet. However, I can also give you two documents. The first is an investigation of the DNA of Eschburg's half-sister. It is established beyond any doubt, and was certified by a notary present at the investigation a year ago at a medical laboratory in Austria. The DNA of the blood and scales of skin found in the course of police inquiries is identical with the half-sister's DNA.

'The second document comes from a police station at Elgin

in Scotland. At my request, Eschburg's half-sister went to the police there yesterday, taking all her documentation with her. She is studying at a boarding school in the vicinity. The police sent me a photograph of her yesterday, which I also add for the record. She is the woman with the crosses on her skin whom you have seen on the video. But above all, she is undoubtedly alive and well.

'To put it another way, your honour and ladies and gentlemen on the judges' bench: you found no body because there was no body. The woman who disappeared never existed. Von Eschburg has been accused of the murder of an installation.'

After this further explanation, there was so much noise that the presiding judge had to adjourn the trial for the day. It was some time before the spectators had left the courtroom.

'That was the strangest day I've ever spent in court,' said Biegler when he was alone with Eschburg. 'But surely it was coincidence that the police officer wanted to torture you, wasn't it?'

'Of course; I couldn't plan that ahead,' said Eschburg. 'But I knew you'd be able to make something of it.'

'But why did you stage it at all? It could have gone wrong,' said Biegler. 'Why go to such lengths? For your sister? For art? For the truth?'

Eschburg looked at him. 'At the end of Titian's life his eyesight was getting worse and worse. He painted his last pictures with his fingers.'

'What do you mean by that?' asked Biegler.

'He couldn't bear to have anything between him and the

pictures any longer. Titian was painting with himself,' said Eschburg. He sounded exhausted; his cheeks were hollow.

Biegler shook his head. 'I hope I'll understand it some time, but at the moment I'm too tired.' He took his coat from the row of hooks and put it on.

'I have one more question, Herr Biegler, a question that a woman once asked me. After all this, can you tell me the answer? What is guilt?'

Biegler looked at the judges' bench. He thought of all the trials he had seen in this courtroom, of the murderers, drug dealers and lost souls he had encountered. 'The police officer here will take you to your cell,' he said. 'You can pack your things there. Sofia will meet you at the exit from the prison. Be nice to her; she really is a good woman.'

When Biegler left the courtroom the journalists outside almost knocked him down. They were all shouting questions at once. A woman in a trouser suit was standing behind them, leaning against the wall. Biegler could see the pale scar on her fore-head. She nodded to him calmly. The woman looked exactly as Eschburg had always described Senja Finks. Biegler was going towards her, but the journalists wouldn't let him through, and by the time he did get to the place where he had seen her, she had disappeared. Biegler shrugged his shoulders. Guilt, he thought, guilt is mankind.

Two weeks later, Sebastian von Eschburg was officially pronounced not guilty of murder.

White

On the other side of the bridge, Eschburg climbed down into the river. The water was cold, and pressed hard against his gumboots. He had his wickerwork bag and his old rod with him, but he was not concentrating on fishing. Sometimes he stopped in the middle of the river to smoke a cigarette. He took the case with the jade stone out of his pocket and ran his fingers over the Japanese characters on the inside. He thought of Sofia and he thought of their son. Soon he'd take the boy fishing with him. He would teach him how to throw out his line, and where to find the shady places in which the trout gathered during the heat of the day, and he would show him how to cook trout on a stick over the fire. He didn't know if he had done things properly, or whether there was in fact any proper way to do things.

We get up every morning, he thought, we live our lives, all the little things that go into them, our work, our hope, making love. We think that what we do is important and that we mean something. We believe we are certain, love is certain, and the society and places in which we live. We believe in all that because otherwise nothing works. But now and then we stop, time tears apart for a moment, and in that moment we understand, all we can see is our own reflections.

Then, gradually, things come back: the laughter of a strange woman in the corridor, afternoons after rain, the smell of wet linen and iris and the dark green moss on the stones. And we go on in the same way as we have always gone on, and as we will always go on again.

The summer fields were bright until they reached the bank. Eschburg was walking downstream. He threw his line far out. For a brief moment the fly lay on the water, gleaming green and red and blue in the sun. Then the river swept it away on the current.